Hannah now gazed again at the window in the A-shaped gable, far above her. Still black. But this is the *only* window that can be seen from our lodge—and it glowed blue, I *know* it did.

Just then the merest shadow appeared inside the high gable window in the Old Sampson Place. Then it was gone. Hannah felt shivers running up and down her already cold and wet spine.

"There...is...*something*...there...all right," Hannah murmured half aloud.

Other books in the

Hannah's
Island

S E R I E S

A Hound for Hannah
The Mystery of the Sunken Steamboat
The Mysterious Stranger

About The Author

Eric E. Wiggin was born on a farm in Albion, Maine in 1939. As a former Maine pastor, Yankee school-teacher, news reporter, and editor of a Maine–published Christian tabloid, Wiggin is intimately familiar with the Pine Tree State and her people. He has strived to model Hannah and Walt after courageous examples of the Maine Christian youth he knows well.

Wiggin's ancestors include Hannah Bradstreet Wiggin, and one of his four granddaughters is Hannah Snyder. But his greatest model for the *Hannah's Island* series is Hannah, mother of the Prophet Samuel, known for her faith and courage in adversity.

Wiggin's ten novels for youth and adults are set in rural or small-town Maine. The woods, fields, and pasture lanes of the Wiggin family farm sloping toward a vast Waldo County bog furnish a natural tapestry for the setting of many of his books.

Author Wiggin now lives in rural Fruitport, Michigan with his wife, Dorothy, and their youngest son, Bradstreet.

The Mysterious Stranger

Eric Wiggin

Emerald Books

P.O. Box 635
Lynnwood, WA 98046

Contents

Chapter One

Spooks

"Something strange is going on in that abandoned house."

Hannah Parmenter found Mrs. Johnson's weird tale upsetting. Hannah had seen the old Sampson place many times from Bald Hill. She found it a rather ordinary old farmhouse. Though it was in need of paint and it hadn't been lived in for years, the house wasn't exactly a tumbledown dump. Papa, in fact, had once talked of buying it and fixing it up.

"There was a light flashing in the upstairs window. I *saw* it," insisted Mrs. Johnson, a summer guest at Beaver Lodge.

Drug dealers? Criminals using the old Sampson place as a hideout, perhaps? Hannah wondered. Silly, she decided. I can't let my imagination run away with itself.

Sampson Cove was the only way to reach the old Sampson place without walking through the woods, Hannah knew. Just last week she'd paddled over there in one of Papa's canoes, but nothing was unusual. Guests at Beaver Lodge, Mama and Papa's small hotel, had several times reported seeing a light there. But always they were satisfied with Papa's explanation that it was only an old mirror in an upstairs hall reflecting the afternoon sun.

Once Hannah had seen it, too. She and Walt were coming back from fishing down the lake. Walt had steered the motorboat a little north of Beaver Island to keep away from a speeding water-skier. When they swung along the west side of the island toward Papa's dock, they saw the Sampson house standing out on the slope of Bald Hill. A bluish light flashed from an attic window, a regular blinking— on-off, on-off, on-off.

"There's *got* to be someone up there turning a light on and off, Papa," Hannah had worried.

"You said 'regular,' " Papa replied. "That tells me it's *mechanical*, not human."

"You mean, like an automatic switch?" Hannah asked, unbelieving.

"The pendulum principle," Papa explained. "A swinging object will continue to swing at the same rate. Suppose the pendulum is a swinging mirror."

"But a mirror wouldn't swing," Hannah insisted. Papa *had* to be wrong in his Sherlock Holmes' explanation.

"It could if it were hung on a long wire," interrupted Mama, who had seen such mirrors in old-fashioned homes. "There's nothing eerie about that."

"But I saw a *face*, too," Mrs. Johnson, who had just returned from a boat ride with her husband, insisted now. "A wild, bearded face, like a crazy old man. And he held a powerful searchlight right in my eyes!"

If the light was in her eyes, how could Mrs. Johnson see the man? Hannah puzzled, but she said nothing. Instead, she said, "I'm goin' over to the cove for a few hours, Mama, if you won't be needing me for the rest of the afternoon."

Though Mrs. Johnson's wild report made her nervous, when Hunter the hound went with her, Hannah was not afraid.

"Have fun," Mama laughed.

"Don't mess with any spooks," teased big brother Walt.

"Cut it out, Walt! C'mon, Hunter."

Hannah and her dog ran to the boathouse for a canoe paddle and a life preserver.

"I'm so happy, Hunter!" Hannah hugged her hound close as they sprawled on the warm sand of Sampson Cove. It was one of those rare midsummer afternoons when Hannah, with nothing to do but loaf, could have the world to herself. She could nap, read, or explore the island. With copies of *Robinson Crusoe* and *Rebecca of Sunnybrook Farm* tucked into an old cloth handbag, Hannah was all set until sundown. But first, she would take a nap.

Sampson Cove was the entrance to the old, abandoned Sampson farm's forty acres of over-grown fields. With its unpainted house and caved-in barn, the Sampson place was the only spot on Beaver Island's nearly four hundred acres that Hannah had never explored. Papa had made it clear that Hannah and Walt were to stay off the Sampson property. Papa had been forced to make one of Adam Sampson's grandsons stop trapping beaver, mink, and otter on Juniper Bog because it inter-fered with Papa and Mama's tourist business. The bog belonged to Papa, but it had once been part of the Sampson farm. So Papa and Mama agreed that trespassing on the farm, even though nobody lived there, might easily lead to trouble.

Sampson Cove was another story. It was the only decent sand beach on Beaver Island, and it was public property.

Hannah rolled over, using Hunter for a pillow. Never mind his fleas. Anyway, they didn't like her shampoo, and Hannah shampooed her thick, strawberry blonde hair every day. No sooner had she dozed off than her hound jumped up, waking her. Hunter shook his handsome head, noisily snapping his hairy, silk-purse ears.

"Enough of that, you silly dog!" Hannah declared. She watched Hunter follow his famous nose into the tangle of wild roses and honeysuckle on the hillside above the beach. She dragged her blanket and cushion over to the old granite steps leading up to the Sampson yard. The steps were covered with moss, leaves, and sticks, as if nobody had climbed up there in many a year. The bottom step tipped down, making a perfect rest for a pillow.

With an old porch cushion beneath her head, Hannah could now contemplate the vast expanse of blue water before her and view the even vaster expanse of green firs and spruces beyond the lake. As she gazed into the distance, Hannah wondered what the world was like far, far to the west where America stretched clear to the broad Pacific. She would not remain on the island forever, Hannah knew. The trip to New York to help Papa sell the rare Lee china had opened to her a world that would continue to call, to beckon, to urge her to explore.

When Hannah awoke, the green firs along the lake had shaded to black in the shadows. The lake now glimmered gold in the slanting last rays of day. Beyond Mt. Kineo, the just departed sun glowed rosy still, making Hannah squint. "I must really have been tired," she yawned. She stretched to swat a mosquito on its evening quest for warm blood.

The patter of animal feet came from the stone steps right above Hannah. Hunter? No. This was not his loping gait.

She turned her head quietly, rolling her eyes. She held her breath, waiting.

A fat, black, ratlike creature tumbled past Hannah. Muskrat? she considered. Hannah sat up, watching the beast trot toward the lake. It had hooves, she was startled to see, like a cow or sheep, only tiny, no larger than a cat's paws. Did such creatures really exist? Seeing is believing, Hannah decided.

Uh, oh! Game's over, Hannah thought. From the thick boughs of a tall hemlock at the water's edge another creature dropped. Its big, feathered body had the bulk of a barnyard rooster, though the wingspan, broad as an eagle's, seemed ample to support this grand gray dive bomber. Hannah squealed in sympathetic terror as a great horned owl, its sharp talons hanging like the landing gear of a jetliner, set its claws into the small, big-bellied beast with the tiny hooves. The animal answered Hannah's squeal with its own shriek, a blood-curdling scream of wild fear.

The owl's wings beat the night air. It rose, fell, rose again, then sank under its burden. Hannah remembered a missionary story about a greedy monkey who preferred to die with its paw inside a gourd trap rather than give up a fisted treasure of pumpkin seeds.

A third creature raced onto the beach. Hunter! He had come down the steps nose down, following the odd animal. Straight for the struggling owl and its strange quarry Hunter ran. The animal was good to eat—Hunter's nose told him that. Hunter had been on the creature's trail first, and he was not about to be robbed of his supper without a fight!

"Hunter!" screamed Hannah. She might as well have been yelling at the stone statue on Laketon's village square. Hunter shot straight for the struggling creature in the owl's talons, tackling it without hesitation.

Chapter Two

The
Oriental Surprise

"You could have got some nasty scars yourself—or even lost an eye, Hannah," Mama admonished. "Large owls have been known to fight people like wildcats."

Less than an hour after Hunter's encounter with the owl and the odd animal, Hannah was back at Beaver Lodge helping Mama clean up a badly hurt hound dog.

"I know, Mama," Hannah whispered, awestruck at what had happened. As she held Hunter down while Mama cleaned his wounds, she realized Mama was right.

"If I hadn't had that canoe paddle handy, I'm sure I'd have gotten clawed, too. But shouldn't we take Hunter to the vet?"

"No need," Mama said, "unless infection sets in. The scratches didn't get into his vital organs—which surprises me."

Hannah realized the danger of catching rabies from wild animals, like those in the *Old Yeller* book.

13

"I guess that owl acted crazy only 'cause he believed Hunter was stealing *his* supper," Hannah mused. "So there's no danger of rabies, I'm sure."

"We've got a real mystery here,"said Mama. She nodded toward the strange dead animal laid on an old newspaper on the porch floor.

"It...it looks *porcine*," said Hannah, practicing a new word she'd read in a nature book.

"Yes," agreed Mama, "it does *look* something like a pig. But it's the oddest one *I* ever saw."

"Maybe it's one of those wild boars, like they hunt in the Great Smoky Mountains in North Carolina." Hannah's interest in nature had caused her to learn many things about American wildlife.

"Hardly," said Mama. "How would such a creature get on our island, here in Moosehead Lake, Maine? This animal appears to be almost an adult. But it's much too small for a boar."

"Well, I've got a hunch," said Hannah pertly.

"What's that?"

"This...this pig is somehow connected to those lights people keep seeing in the Sampson house— and to the bearded man Mrs. Johnson says she saw."

"Think so?" Mama was not convinced.

"Where are you going with that wild pig?" Papa asked Hannah half an hour later, as she hurried toward the pasture with the pig in a shovel and a flashlight in the other hand.

"Goin' t' bury it," Hannah said in disgust. "Mama said to get it out of the house."

To tell the truth, Hannah had no desire to trudge across a pasture at night to bury a dead animal she'd brought home and which Hunter would surely dig back up as soon as she let him off his chain. She had planned to leave it by the pasture gate in hopes the owl would find it that night. If it was still there next morning, she'd have time to bury it before breakfast.

"I don't think that's a good idea," mused Papa, who had seen the critter when Hannah first came home, dragging Hunter, whining and bleeding, by his collar.

"You don't?"

"There is something strange going on here," said Papa, rubbing his chin. "Take it into the milk room," he added firmly. "Scrub it good with a brush and chlorine solution to disinfect it. Then bring it into the kitchen. It can stay in the fridge wrapped in an old dish towel for a day or two while we try to figure out what it is. Mama won't like it, but I'll tell her what we're doing."

❋ ❋ ❋ ❋ ❋ ❋ ❋

Oriental, thought Hannah. She helped Walt carry luggage for the dark-haired woman who had just arrived with her blond husband on Beaver Island. "Marie Janeki," the tag on the woman's luggage read. "You may call me Marie," she replied pleasantly when Hannah referred to her as "Mrs. Janeki." Marie's accent, Hannah thought, is rather pretty.

Pretty, too, was Marie's smile, with her emerald green eyes shining beneath her straight black hair as pearl white teeth flashed bright between naturally ruby lips.

I'm going to like this guest, Hannah thought. She wished to ask the woman a few things about herself, but Hannah decided it might not be polite.

✴ ✴ ✴ ✴ ✴ ✴ ✴

"I love your island, Hannah," Mrs. Janeki remarked two evenings later, laughing with delight.

"I love it, too—but then, it's my home," Hannah said modestly. She stopped at the foot of the porch steps to pet Hunter and kiss his wet nose. Then she hurried up to where Mrs. Janeki sat primly rocking in a high-backed rocker.

"It gets cool here in the evening," Hannah continued. "Can I get you a sweater, Mrs. Jan...? I mean Marie."

"I'm all set," said Marie. Smiling, she reached under her chair and fished out her sweater, which she'd folded and placed there.

"Actually I live on an island myself—Manhattan," she chuckled.

"Manhattan Island is the business district of New York City," Hannah brighty said. "I visited there last year. But I didn't know people *live* there."

"There are many apartments in Manhattan." Marie paused, as if remembering. "America is such a marvelous country," she said, breathing in the fresh woodland air.

"Where...where are you from, really?" Marie had opened up by suggesting that she was not born in America.

"Oh, I've lived in New York since I was a little girl," Marie giggled. "My parents brought me here from Vietnam, though. My husband's family is from Poland. But we are all Americans now."

"Vietnam's in southeast Asia, isn't it?" Hannah thought she knew, but she had to ask.

"Yes," Marie agreed. "I've been back once, with my mother when I was about your age. It's a very different way of life."

Hannah hurried inside, where she helped herself to a glass of milk from the family refrigerator. No pig. Maybe Papa's buried it, Hannah thought, noticing that her porcine creature was missing. About time, she decided.

Papa had had a large hotel type of refrigerator installed in the supply room when he'd had the new wing built. Mama kept leftover desserts there, and she'd told her guests to help themselves whenever they wanted an evening snack. So Hannah was not surprised, a few minutes later, to see Marie slip quietly into the supply room.

"What...is...this...*pig* doing here?" Marie squealed.

Hannah hurried into the supply room.

Marie had closed the refrigerator and was standing under the bright florescent light holding the pig with the cloth it had been wrapped in now carelessly unwound. Marie smiled when she saw Hannah.

"It...it's *not* supposed to be in *that* fridge," Hannah declared. Then it dawned on her that Marie was not upset. In fact, she was smiling.

"It's darling," Marie murmured. "So cute. Did your dog kill this poor Vietnamese miniature pot-bellied pig?"

"Vietnamese pig? Why...why, it was killed by an owl," Hannah stammered. "I'll take it," she added quickly.

"Please do." Marie smiled and held it out.

Embarrassed, Hannah hurried to the family refrigerator, but she found no room for the pig. Walt had placed the can of evening milk from Molly the family cow there.

"I think it's time we got rid of that horrid thing, like I asked two days ago," Mama snapped, stepping into the kitchen. "Your father has taken a picture of it, so we *don't* need to keep a cadaver in the refrigerator!"

"Mama, I'll bury it right away. But..." Hannah stopped. Mrs. Janeki thinks it's cute, isn't what I want to say, exactly, she thought. "Mama, this is a Vietnamese potbellied pig," Hannah cried instead.

"Nonsense! Vietnam's halfway around the world."

"Yes, but...."

"Hannah is right, Mrs. Parmenter," said a pleasant voice. "I've seen them in Vietnam—and also in the Bronx Zoo in New York."

"Well...well then," said Mama, surprised at Marie Janeki's confidence. "I guess we can keep it until Papa gets back from Laketon. But it can't go back in the refrigerator used by our guests. Hannah, please move the milk can. I don't know whatever possessed Walter to place a dead pig in the big fridge and leave it all unwrapped!"

Chapter Three

A Detective
on Horseback

"Here, boy!" Hannah cried, whistling into the mist that shrouded the hillside pasture above Papa's barn one morning in August. "Tweet!" she whistled again. Hunter, standing with his forepaws on the cedar bars of the pasture gate, trembled in excitement as he waited with his mistress for Ebony to appear.

Hannah loved these misty Maine mornings on Beaver Island. She sat, one leg looped across the top bar, petting a quivering Hunter with one hand as she steadied her new Western saddle on her knee with the other. The dull "donk, donk, donk" of Molly's cowbell came from somewhere in the fog as the family cow grabbed a few breakfast mouthfuls of timothy and sweet clover before Walt came out to milk her.

"Here, Ebony," Hannah sang out, whistling again. A rumble of heavy hooves from far up the hillside toward the spring told Hannah that her black stallion had obeyed. Saddling a large horse

19

was a rugged chore for a girl not quite a teen. But Hannah had practiced this maneuver dozens of times. Since the sale of the Lee china had given her money for a new saddle, Hannah no longer rode Ebony bareback.

The horse now trotted up, steaming and snuffing, and he nuzzled up to Hannah at once. "Good feller," she chirped, reaching into a pocket of her jeans for a handful of sugar cubes. Hannah let her horse savor his sugar, then, "Hunter, bring 'im around!" she commanded. At once Hannah's hound squirreled beneath the bottom bar. Nipping gently at Ebony's heels, Hunter urged the horse to step sideways until the grand black steed stood alongside the bars. Hannah tossed the horse blanket in place, then immediately clapped the saddle on top of it. Jumping off the bars, Hannah cinched the saddle tight, then grabbed Ebony's halter, which she had hung on a fence post.

Hannah had not been back to Sampson Cove since the day Hunter had tangled with the great horned owl, fighting with this feathered felon of the forest over a Vietnamese potbellied pig. Hannah did not share Mrs. Johnson's superstition about the lights flashing from the Sampson house. But Hannah had found this creature many thousands of miles from its home, which added a puzzling new angle to the mystery of the old Sampson place. Hannah felt there just might be a connection.

This morning Mama had given Hannah several hours of freedom from helping to wait on guests at Beaver Lodge. So Hannah decided to investigate from the safety of a saddled stallion, with faithful Hunter trotting alongside. She determined to take the only other approach to the old Sampson place—

Hannah's special private trail up Bald Hill. The old Sampson place was a legend the length of Moosehead Lake. The house was built toward the end of the nineteenth century—a substantial New England farmhouse, spacious, and with a solid slate roof that still kept the interior dry.

Old Adam Sampson had died years ago, after many years of running a large island farm to supply logging camps just north of the big lake with vegetables, milk, and fresh eggs. Adam and his children had sold most of Beaver Island in three separate pieces to investors who had later built Beaver Lodge. These investors eventually sold the lodge to Hannah's parents, Harry and Sandy Parmenter, as a tourist home.

Then the Sampson children had all died, leaving the big house, a barn in ruins, and such a tangle of claims by grandchildren and great-grandchildren for the house and remaining forty acres that, said Papa, "Even King Solomon and all the lawyers in Philadelphia couldn't untangle the mess." Papa had tried unsuccessfully to buy the Sampson house, with the idea of renting it to an overflow of paying guests.

From time to time a boatload of Sampson descendants would spend a weekend at their grandfather Adam's old house. Then there had been the day when Hannah and Walt discovered Sam Sampson camping next to Juniper Bog, where he had been trapping beaver without Papa's permission. One of Papa's guests had had a hunting dog injured by Sam's traps. Sam had been mad as a wet skunk after Hannah helped Papa gather up all his traps, using Hunter's keen nose to sniff out the bait.

But now there was no boat in Sampson Cove—Hannah had buzzed past there last evening in Papa's motorboat to make sure. Still, after the pig episode, Hannah was not about to venture ashore. She shuddered to think about it even now. Where *did* that cute little pig come from? Hannah pondered. What's it doing on Beaver Island?

Hannah trotted Ebony across the pasture toward the gap in the old stone wall just as the morning sun began to melt the mist from the hillside. She lowered the bars that led to the forest road across the island, then guided her horse through. "Git-up!" she cried, swinging back into the saddle, and Ebony raced off, galloping over the pine and hemlock needles carpeting the forest floor.

Hannah stayed low, hanging onto Ebony's long mane with one hand to avoid branches crisscrossing the old logging road. A family of partridges shot suddenly across the road, their wings beating the morning air with such furor that Hannah laughed aloud at their silly terror.

"Whoa!" Suddenly Hannah braced herself in the stirrups and tightened the reins.

Ebony halted, and Hunter halted beside him.

Another winged creature crossed the road just as girl and horse reached the head of Juniper Bog. It was a horned owl, and on mighty wings its bulky body mounted into the air at a steep angle. A hapless bullfrog, the nightbird's late breakfast, was struggling in cruel talons behind. The owl disappeared into the thick branches of a black spruce. Here, Hannah knew, once it devoured the frog, the owl would nod away the daytime hours until dusk and hunger drove it forth to hunt the night away.

"A-r-r-r-r-r-r-r!" Hunter appraised the situation.

Looking down, Hannah could see the hair stand up on her dog's neck. His teeth were bared, and his eyes were narrowed to slits.

"We've seen this guy before, haven't we feller?" Hannah remarked grimly.

"O-o-o-o-oh!" Hunter squealed, as much from his still-sore scars as from fear, Hannah was sure.

Hannah would no more urge Ebony to pass under that spruce tree than if she'd just seen a hungry wild lynx waiting to spring on her from a limb. Instead, she turned Ebony into a thicket of young firs at the base of Bald Hill. She let her horse pick his own way among these small trees until they broke into the trail again uphill from the black spruce.

Chapter Four

A Pig's Dinner

A series of twists and turns brought them out of the forest, where a field of two or three acres stretched across the crown of the hill. The field was crowded with low-bush wild blueberries loaded with ripening fruit.

"I'll remind Mama that the berries are about ripe," Hannah said, speaking as much to herself as to her horse and hound.

Hunter stopped to sniff at a heap of animal droppings larger than deer dung and gathered in a pile much too large to have been left by a raccoon.

"Hunter!" Hannah cried, as the hound began to follow his nose over the top of the hill.

Hunter stopped. "O-o-o-o-o-o," he complained.

"Come back here!"

Papa's loggers had seen a black bear on the island only last winter. Though Papa had said black bears aren't dangerous unless you mess with their cubs, Hannah had no desire to meet one alone and without a gun. She had heard that bears eat blueberries, so she decided to bring Walt's shotgun

24

when she and Mama had returned to fill their buckets with pie berries.

Hannah let Ebony walk among the stones and stumps that jutted out in the blueberry barren as they moved across the hill. Presently they reached the pinnacle. From her perch in the saddle, Hannah scanned the shoreline. Far below, the copper roof of Beaver Lodge gleamed in the morning sun. Hannah then noticed Uncle Joe Boudreau's plywood replica of the *President Lincoln* steamboat slowly paddling toward Beaver Island from Laketon.

Hey, didn't Mama say that Uncle Joe's bringing a boatload of overnight guests this morning? Hannah asked herself. Usually she'd have left at once to be home when her uncle arrived. But Hannah had learned nothing useful toward unraveling her mystery so far this morning, and she was determined not to go home until she learned something. Like Papa, who had asked questions all over Laketon, Hannah simply had no idea where the strange oriental pig had come from.

Hannah now turned toward the twin chimneys of the old Sampson place. The slate roof was covered with mossy lichens, and knee-deep weeds crowded the back door. A grape arbor that once held a vine next to the kitchen wing had rotted and collapsed, and the vines had nearly swallowed that end of the house. Gulls perched on the chimneys made it apparent that no fires were burning in the stoves downstairs. A TV antenna, which a Sampson family heir had installed many years ago during a brief attempt at making the old house a home, teetered crazily from its bracket on one chimney. An old windcharger, which once supplied electricity for the TV set, had fallen off its tower and lay in a rusty heap in the backyard.

Hannah could not see the front windows of the house, and since brush had crowded in on the side facing the lake, she could see very little of the yard, either. From up here, the trees along the waterfront hid all of Sampson Cove.

"Not much to look at, guys," Hannah told Ebony and Hunter. "Let's move along."

Hannah slapped the reins, then pointed Ebony across the blueberry field to where a broken-down rail fence and rock wall marked the edge of what Hannah decided had once been a cow pasture. A gap in the fence showed where a gate had rotted off. Hannah decided to investigate. *Perhaps there's an old road or path I can follow for a closer look,* she told herself.

Halfway to the old gate opening, Hannah reined Ebony in. Two furry, round-eared black creatures waddled from behind a large boulder halfway between Hannah and the gate.

"Cute," she said under her breath. "Twins?" Then, *What am I saying?* raced through her mind. She remembered thinking that the Vietnamese pig also was cute. The attack from the air had changed her pleasant afternoon at the cove into one of terror.

These animals seemed intent on reaching the shade of a huge, lone oak that stood next to the old stone wall. It suddenly occurred to Hannah that the pile of dung among the blueberries had been left by a berry-hungry bear—no doubt about it.

Hunter now sprang into action. His curiosity was equal to Hannah's, though he lacked her good sense as he raced toward the bear cubs.

"*Hun-terrr!*" screamed Hannah.

The hound braked to a halt—none too soon. He *had* learned to obey—the owl had reinforced a lesson this hound had received a couple of years earlier with a porcupine.

An adult black bear appeared from behind the boulder. She reared onto her hind legs, roaring in wrath. The cubs, not quite to the tree, froze in their tracks.

Hunter froze, too, then slowly backed away.

Hannah lay down on Ebony's neck. "Easy boy, steady," she commanded, whispering into his ear, even as she pulled the reins so tight his bit must have hurt terribly, she later realized.

Mrs. Bruin now came down on all fours. With a warning snarl in parting to Hunter, the mother bear hurried off to collect her cubs.

What happened next surprised Hannah more than meeting the bears in the blueberry patch. The weeds and grass beneath the stalwart oak suddenly came alive with small piggy bodies, some black, others snowwhite. Their potbellies bouncing ridiculously as they scampered through the gate, Vietnamese miniature pigs, dozens of them, scurried madly through the gap and disappeared into an overgrown path in the direction of the old Sampson place.

❋ ❋ ❋ ❋ ❋ ❋ ❋

"A pig's dinner," chuckled Papa, when later that morning Hannah told him what she'd seen in the blueberry field. "And I'd guess they didn't want to become a bear's lunch. Pigs will gather under oak trees to root for acorns in last winter's dead leaves."

"But Papa, there were so many!" Hannah protested.

Papa shrugged. "Two or two hundred, there's little difference. My guess is, someone dumped a pair on Beaver Island. They simply holed up in that abandoned farmhouse and multiplied. They'd have few natural enemies here."

"But Papa..."

He held up his hand. "Let me show you what your Uncle Joe brought." Papa picked up a recent copy of the *Bangor Daily News*, Maine's largest newspaper. "Foxcroft Man Has Novel Piggery," read the backpage headline.

"Would you believe it?" Papa remarked. "Feller over Foxcroft way is raising Vietnamese potbellied pigs to sell as pets. He plans to deliver them to pet stores all across New England once he gets his stock built up."

"But *what* are these pigs doing on *our* island?" Hannah was now completely exasperated. Papa's explanation and Uncle Joe's newspaper article only went in circles, it seemed to Hannah. "So now we know people raise these creatures as pets. We still have a mystery!"

"How did that two-foot Florida alligator get into Moosehead Lake last summer?" interrupted Walt, yawning. "Who cares?"

Hannah knew that that mystery had not been solved, either, though the game warden had guessed that a summer tourist had raised it until it got too big for their aquarium, then simply tossed it into the lake.

"My concern is, how are we going to get rid of them before they multiply more and become pests," Papa said. "Sometimes, Hannah, I think you let your imagination run away with you."

Hannah had no reply. *Men!* she thought to herself. They never think I know what I'm talking about.

Chapter Five

The Porcelain Pig

Pigs! Hannah rolled over in bed as she tried to sleep. *Pigs!* That was all she could think about. The mystery of the pig at Sampson Cove had become many small pigs, dozens, hundreds, maybe, scurrying into the underbrush on the hill behind the old Sampson place.

Every attempt at solving the riddle seemed to bring Hannah the scorn of her family. Oh, no one had made fun of her, exactly. But Mama had called that poor dead miniature Vietnamese potbellied pig a *cadaver*, like in a morgue, although Marie Janeki had said it was *cute*.

And big brother Walt? Someone had once found an alligator in Moosehead Lake, way too far north for such a southern swamp reptile to survive the winter. How it had ended up there, nobody knew. Walt's estimation of the pigs, like the alligator, was, "Who cares?" Like Mama, Walt certainly did *not* understand mysteries.

Hannah tossed in her bed again, remembering

Papa's remarks about the pigs. Papa had tried to be helpful at first, even suggesting that for a few days Hannah keep the pig she had pounded out of the owl's claws with an oar. "You fought like a tiger to get him, honey," Papa had said that day he told her to put the pig in the refrigerator. "I guess the least we can do is find out what that critter is," he had added, patting her on the head.

Papa had snapped a picture of the pig and showed it to several business friends in Laketon, but no one knew what it was or where it could have come from.

Only Marie Janeki, the Vietnamese woman from New York, had ever seen one. Now there was this newspaper article about a man raising them on a farm near Foxcroft. That seemed to clinch it for Papa and Walt. Potbellied pigs are pets, and people do strange and cruel things with pets when they tire of them.

Papa might be right, of course. Twice Hannah and Walt had found half-grown puppies on Beaver Island, abandoned by an inconsiderate boater who used the island to dump unwanted pets.

But there's a whole *herd* of pigs up behind Bald Hill! Hannah protested into the silent night. Her room was lit with moonlight now as the night wind scudded the clouds away, exposing the setting moon over Mt. Kineo to the west.

Hannah rolled out of bed. Huddling in her chair by the window, she peered down the lake. Only a light or two shined from the cottages along the shore. The village of Laketon was dark except for the row of streetlights that marched uphill from the waterfront and the traffic signal blinking off and on at the intersection of Main Street and State Road.

Hannah turned now, peering along Beaver Island's waterfront, toward the north. Here, a majestic pine, its long-needled branches tossing black in the night breeze, hid the old Sampson house from view. Then the wind moved the pine's limbs, and Hannah caught a glimpse of a glow of light. She stared—there it was again.

Hannah had seen the windows of both Beaver Lodge and the old Sampson house more than once in the afternoon sun as she motored southeast toward home, the setting sun at her back. The windowpanes had shone golden on those occasions, Hannah remembered. But the time she had seen the same light that had worried Mrs. Johnson, it had been a bluish flash of light. This seemed to be a bluish glow. What would moonlight reflecting off glass look like, anyway?

Hannah slipped silently to her door and scooted into the hall. She hurried up the narrow stairs toward Walt's room on the third floor to get a look from higher up. The door was ajar. Since Walt seemed to be sleeping, Hannah slid in and knelt by the window, which also faced the tall pine.

"What y' doin' in my bedroom, Sis?" Walt stirred, propping up on one elbow.

"Come see!" Hannah excitedly pointed toward the pine.

"I can't believe this," Walt grumbled sleepily. But he rolled out of bed anyway and struggled to the window.

"There it is!" Hannah pointed as the pine, bent by the breeze, revealed a glimmer of light plainer than from her second-floor room.

"So? Just the moon striking the gable window of that old house."

"But it's blue!"

"Moonlight does funny things to old glass," Walt yawned, confident of himself. "I'm goin' back to bed."

Ten minutes later Hannah, in sneakers and a denim jacket over her pajamas, slipped to the waterfront, her hound close behind. Glad for Hunter's company, she scurried onto Papa's dock, then turned to view the effect of moonlight on the windows of Beaver Lodge. They glimmered silver, not gold, certainly not blue.

It was a troublesome trip to the old pine, with only the moon for a light as Hannah picked her way along the shoreline. Hannah tripped over tree roots and stubbed her toes on rocks until they were raw and sore. Nearly there, Hannah waded in knee-deep lake water past a large boulder, Hunter swimming at her side. She used a loose rock as a stepping-stone, but it flipped beneath her foot and she fell completely in. Not bothering to wring the water from her pajamas, Hannah at last struggled ashore beyond the pine.

"C'mon, Hunt," she whispered.

Hunter had his own way of dealing with water, and he shook, loudly snapping his flopears, spraying Hannah with more water. Pushing now through a tangle of blackberry brambles with the protection of a dry pine limb, Hannah at last emerged where she could view the gable end of the Sampson house.

Odd, thought Hannah. The gable window was now dark. As Hannah peered back past the pine, she could see that those windows of Beaver Lodge facing the lake still caught the silver mooonbeams. But since this window was at the end of the Sampson house, it did not face the moon. Then why was it lighted when I watched it from home? Hannah puzzled.

Hannah now gazed again at the window in the A-shaped gable far above her. Still black. But this is the *only* window that can be seen from our lodge— and it glowed blue, I *know* it did.

Just then the merest shadow appeared inside the high gable window in the old Sampson place. Then it was gone. Hannah felt shivers running up and down her already cold and wet spine. "There is *something* there all right," Hannah murmured half aloud.

"R-r-r-r-r-uff!" agreed Hunter.

"Saw it too, did y', boy?" Hannah turned and hurried toward the safety of Beaver Lodge.

"Dear Marie,..."

Hannah chewed on her ballpoint pen and stared at the postcard in front of her. It was a photo of Times Square at night, and she knew she would treasure it always, for it helped her remember her own trip to New York as well as her Oriental friend there. Mrs. Janeki had written to Hannah on the back of this card. Hannah had replied the same day, but so far she had not received another letter.

How Hannah had enjoyed Marie's stay at Beaver Lodge! What fun to have an adult friend you could talk to on a first-name basis! Papa had once said, "You're almost a woman, Hannah." And being a woman meant you called other women by their first names, sharing secrets, laughing at their jokes.

"Now we've got Vietnamese potbellied pigs all over the place on Bald Hill," Hannah wrote. "And I know someone is staying at that old house—you remember, the abandoned farmhouse around the point from our lodge. I *saw* him, and Hunter saw him, too.

"For now I'm *not* telling anyone but you. Papa knows there are pigs up there, but he believes they're just pests or rodents. He wants to trap them and move them off the island. Walter would even *shoot* them. Can you believe it? So I've *got* to learn what's going on by myself. Your friend, Hannah Parmenter"

Two weeks later Hannah was at the Laketon post office, picking up the family's mail. A package twice the size of a shoe box was addressed to her. The return address read:

M. Janeki
137 West End Blvd.
New York, NY 10099

Before unwrapping the package's contents, Hannah unfolded the letter that lay on top of a pile of packing material. Marie had written a short note:

"Here is a little gift from Vietnam that I think you'll find rather cute. Enjoy it.

"Your Papa is right. Potbellied pigs do multiply very fast. But if he's going to catch them, he should remember that fine specimens are worth $10,000 to $15,000 in pet stores in New York. Even ordinary ones bring $50, and folks here buy them as fast as they become available. They must be domesticated, of course.

"As for the blue light in the window next door, there are many possible explanations. I think you're right that someone is staying in that house. But I'm sure they'd be much more friendly if you simply took Walter or one of your parents and knocked on the front door. Regards, Marie"

Maybe Marie's right, Hannah considered. There's nothing to lose in making friends with our neighbors even if they are a bit odd. But then... Hannah remembered how the Sampsons had seemed hostile the couple of times they had visited the island. Perhaps I'd better learn a little more about what's going on over there before I just march up and introduce myself, Hannah thought. She dropped Marie's letter into the cloth shopping bag she had brought for the mail and began to unwrap her gift on a post office table.

An arched top of a brilliant jade green soon appeared in the packing. It had a slot, as though to drop coins through. Hannah tapped it with her fingernails, savoring every moment of unwrapping this mysterious gift. It gave off a nice, musical clink.

Porcelain, she decided.

More packing came out. *A large bank?*

Still more packing went into the trash can beneath the table. Hannah now lifted out Marie's gift.

"A porcelain potbellied pig!" she squealed. It was the most beautiful piece of glazed crockery Hannah had ever seen, fully as big as the half-grown pig she had taken from the owl! Except for its green color, every detail was perfect.

Chapter Six

A Dog's Supper

"You're entirely too much off your feed lately, bear breath!" Hannah scratched Hunter's lop-ears as he rolled his languid brown eyes guiltily up to meet her green ones. "Whatever have you been eating?"

Labor Day had passed on Beaver Island, and except for weekends, there were few hotel guests at Beaver Lodge. It would be a couple of weeks yet before retired couples came to enjoy the fall colors around Moosehead Lake. Partridge, duck, and deer hunting seasons followed the fall color season, and Hunter would need to be kept chained during the rest of the fall so as not to bother guests.

Hannah thought it only fair that Hunter be permitted to roam for the remaining two weeks of summer. "A dog by himself won't worry the deer herd," "Papa had said. "He'll catch a few rabbits, but that'll be that many fewer to eat our garden next summer and destroy our apple trees this winter," he observed.

Right after Labor Day, Hannah and Walt had plunged into their schoolwork. Since they would have a hotel full of guests all fall, brother and sister, who were home schooled, needed to work ahead of schedule.

Hannah had begun her science project in the middle of August, right after she had gone shopping with Aunt Theresa at the Skowhegan mall. She had bought a precision scales, planning to feed Hunter purely on scientific principles, keeping careful records for her assignment.

For several weeks, Hannah had weighed out Hunter's dog food, recording every ounce that he ate. She had even formulated her own hypothesis: "A dog's food intake will increase in direct proportion to his daily hours of exercise." For a couple of weeks, Hannah's hypothesis seemed to be proving true. If Hunter ran with her to bring Molly to the barn for milking or followed Papa around the fields for an hour, his food intake increased in proportion, and so on.

So letting him run round the clock would make her hound ravenous for food, Hannah theorized. She had overspent herself in August, and Hannah was concerned that Hunter's new appetite might cause him to eat more than she could afford. And when she let him run during daytime hours only, his appetite *did* increase a great deal.

So, "What *are* you doing for food?" Hannah asked, puzzled.

Hunter was not sick, his coat was sleek, and he was fat as ever. But he would only nibble at his dog food, then go to sleep in the sun. And he was not losing weight. Hannah weighed him daily, only to find that his fat, lazy belly was becoming muscle by healthy exercise. Oh, he picked up horse nettles and burdock burrs enough. His coat got dirty daily, and this kept Hannah busy carding and combing. And the fleas! Flea powder, flea soap, flea spray— even a flea collar didn't seem to help. Hannah consoled herself, though, that when the cold and snow came, one good bath would keep him flea-free all winter.

But, "*What* are you eating?" she asked again. Hannah could not believe that eating skinny rabbits and bony squirrels could keep her hound's weight up.

One afternoon the fall sun's low rays slanted back into Hunter's home under the kitchen porch. Hannah peered in. The downy white tail of a bunny caught her eye, and she plopped onto her belly, dragging her head and shoulders inside for a better look.

"Look at this!" Hannah cried, spying Papa coming from the barn half an hour later. She laid out five rabbit tails, three gray squirrel tails, a red squirrel tail, and a chipmunk tail.

"Quite a collection!" Papa said in surprise. He rubbed his chin thoughtfully. "No wonder we haven't seen squirrels all summer. And I've been blaming ol' Tige, the barn cat. But I guess *he* gets his fill just by killing haymow mice."

"And just see this—pigs' toenails—50 or 60, at least! How many do you suppose Hunter's killed?" Hannah held up a coffee can into which she'd ladeled the yucky things with an old spoon, careful not to touch them with her fingers.

"Count 'em," Papa said matter-of-factly, secretly glad that Hunter was ridding the island of pests he figured could overrun their land and spoil his business. "Divide by four. Pigs have four legs apiece, you know."

"You're *so* smart," Hannah teased. "I already have. The silly hound has eaten maybe 15 Vietnamese pigs!"

Hannah's ears burned red as she recalled what Marie had written about potbellied pigs being valuable. She guessed she'd better tell Papa about the letter—and the blue light in the window. Tomorrow is Saturday, and I'm not expected to do schoolwork, Hannah silently told herself. Snapping Hunter to his chain so that he could not run that night, Hannah determined to take action the next morning.

Chapter Seven

Who Is My Neighbor?

"Where are you going with your brother's shotgun?" Mama frowned, waiting.

"Bear hunting, Mama," Hannah chuckled. "I've already asked Walt."

Though Hannah felt it was wrong not to answer Mama's question, she still could not tell Mama what was up.

"Well, all right," Mama agreed. Her voice exhibited a note of worry, even though she knew Hannah was teasing about hunting a bear.

Mama and Hannah had spent an afternoon in August berrying on Bald Hill until their buckets were full. It took two trips across the steep places to bring their brimming buckets down without spilling the blueberries. Hannah had told Mama about the bear and her cubs, but bears did not scare Mama.

"If we worried about every bear that ever visited a blueberry patch, we'd never eat another berry," Mama stoutly insisted. Mama had been a city girl, but like many Maine families, hers had gone berrying in the countryside each summer when she was a child.

Both Mama and Hannah agreed, however, that Hunter should go along to protect them. But they kept him chained to an old stump. "We can't have that hound deciding he wants to play tag with those cubs," Mama affirmed.

Hannah found three shotgun shells for Walt's 12-gauge on the shelf by the cellar stairs and dropped them into her jacket pocket. She grabbed Hunter's leash from its hook by the kitchen door, then hurried outside.

Papa did not require permission to use firearms on Beaver Island on days that there were no guests around. He had three rules—no loaded guns indoors, don't point a gun at anything you don't intend to shoot, and use common sense. This last rule covered about everything else, such as not pointing a gun at your toe and setting your gun down before climbing over a fence.

To tell the truth, though Hannah had fired Walt's shotgun at a target until her shoulder was black and blue from its kick, she had no interest in killing animals. She could accept that Hunter killed to eat, of course and Hannah could eat what Walt or Papa brought home.

Hannah had told Mama truthfully that she was going to *hunt*. But she had no plans to *kill*. Yet something strange, perhaps sinister was going on in back of Bald Hill, and Hannah felt she ought to carry a gun if she was going to let Hunter's sharp nose lead her into possible trouble.

Of course, Hannah might have told Papa first. But after finding those pigs' hooves in Hunter's home only yesterday, Hannah determined to find a few more pieces of the puzzle before she asked her parents or Walt to help her unravel the mystery.

"C'mon boy!" Though Hunter was used to being chained at night, he wasn't used to being on a leash when he roamed the farm and forest with Hannah. He soon began to zigzag, trying to follow a rabbit trail that Hannah could plainly see led beneath the henhouse.

Hannah dragged her complaining dog away from the rabbit scent, then she brought from her pocket a handful of tiny hooves and one tiny tail, which she'd found under the kitchen porch. She held them up to Hunter's nose.

The effect was electric. His nose twitched, his tail stood up, his entire body trembled with excitement.

"Like that, huh? Now I want you to show me where you've been getting your dinner!"

Hannah was not surprised that Hunter ran straight for the old logging road that crossed the island. But after passing through the pines and firs around the base of Bald Hill, Hunter ignored the trail up toward the blueberry barren. Instead, he turned into a narrow but well-defined path that looked to Hannah like one of those meandering trails Papa called deer paths.

Skirting the edge of Juniper Bog with Hunter, and Hannah was soon glad she had worn her stout L.L. Bean boots for the jaunt. Here and there muddy water from the low clay ground covered the trail, and thick-growing, razor-sharp swale grass whipped at her boot tops.

Hunter now nosed his way into thickets where Hannah had to crouch, careful to handle her shotgun so that she did not get water inside the barrel or fall facedown in the mud.

All at once the trail disappeared, and tracks seemed to run in all directions beneath the over-spreading alders and hazelnut bushes. Hunter strained at his leash, and Hannah at once decided that his nose had picked up something. She tied him to a beech tree, which towered above the rest of the nut-bearing thicket.

Hannah took a closer look. The tracks were tiny hoofprints, like deer, only smaller. Here and there in the underbrush the snuffing and grunting of greedy snouts devouring hazelnuts, beechnuts, and alder-berries left no doubt but that the potbellied pigs Hannah had seen weeks earlier on the slope facing the old Sampson place had come down to Papa's bogland for a late-summer feast. With every step, now, a pig, or several pigs, scurried into the brush, their dragging bellies telling Hannah that Beaver Island was a porker's land of plenty.

"You 'n I have seen enough," Hannah told Hunter, unhitching him from the tree. "No, you're *not* eating a pig for dinner today, you rascal."

Instead of following the meandering pig path back toward Bald Hill, Hannah pushed directly for high ground, taking the shortest route to the open logging road.

"I wonder?" Hannah asked herself moments later as she stood on the dry road above the bog. She broke open Walt's single-shot gun, then loaded it with birdshot, a round that she knew would do no damage except at close range. She aimed at a stump and pulled the trigger.

The gun roared. The pigs squealed. There must be more than a hundred, Hannah thought, as what seemed like an endless stream of tiny porkers with bobbing bellies tore out of the path from the alder patch, crossed the road, and disappeared into a fir thicket, racing up Bald Hill.

An angry roar in the road directly behind Hannah made her blood chill. As she tightened her knuckles around Hunter's leash, Hannah noticed that the hair on her hound's neck stood up.

"R-r-r-r-r-r-r!" was Hunter's response, but he made no move to disobey his mistress's firm "Stay!"

Cautiously Hannah turned around—to face a hairy, red-eyed creature standing upright, like the she-bear in defense of her cubs. Hannah quietly observed the angry one who had threatened her. He was male, and he wasn't a bear—bears don't swear.

The fellow cursed again. "Are you goin' to blow me away with that shootin' iron o' yourn, missy?" he asked. "I bin missin' some o' m' pigs. I guess you 'n yer dog's t' blame fer that," he added, punctuating his accusations with more profanity.

"A gentleman does *not* swear at a lady." Hannah was unsure she'd said the right thing, but she had to say *something*.

"You goin' t' shoot me?" he asked again.

Only then did Hannah realize she was unconsciously pointing the gun straight at the man's chest. *He's not thinking straight if he thinks I can shoot him with a single-barrel shotgun that's just been fired.* Aloud, she said, "Not unless you come closer."

The odor of a mixture of alcohol, tobacco, and unwashed man now reached Hannah's nose. But her compassion rode over her disgust, and she felt only pity—pity mixed with the fear that the man might be dangerous. She looked him up and down, sizing him up. *Hermit* was all she could conclude as she noticed the waist-length, dirty hair and the beard that fell even lower. The man wore a billed cap pulled down to his eyebrows, so Hannah could see little of his angry face.

"Your pigs were on my Papa's land, sir," she added politely.

This only brought on more swearing.

"My grandfather, Adam Sampson, he owned this island," the man raved. "An' us Sampsons, we *shtill* own it, all 'cept the other side o' yer ol' man's pasture fence. You tell your Papa, missy, that I'm goin' to sue him. Effen Harry Parmenter wants t' stay out o' jail, he'll give me that fancy tourist hotel to pay fer all the timber he's stole frum me!"

"I'll tell him, sir." Hannah was trembling now. But she stood, her feet rooted to the logging road, until Mr. Sampson was out of sight up the hill. Then she ran all the way home.

❋ ❋ ❋ ❋ ❋ ❋ ❋

"Hannah's right," Walt insisted. "I didn't believe her at first, but there was a bluish light in that attic window nearly all night. I could see it from my window whenever the wind moved the pine tree."

The Parmenter family was having a family council around the kitchen table right after Hannah returned with her report of meeting the mysterious, angry stranger.

"Well, we've got a neighbor, and he's been here long enough to get his piggery well established," Papa put in. "That means he's been sneaking around, coming and going when the rest of us are asleep. Likely he keeps his boat out of sight in the bushes where his lawn used to be. Who knows what else might be going on over there?" Papa was indignant.

"Incidentally..." Papa looked searchingly at Hannah. "Did you recognize this Mr. Sampson? Have you seen him before?"

"I couldn't see much of his face. But he does look sorta like that guy who was so mad when we pulled his beaver traps."

"Sam Sampson?" Mama wondered.

"We'll soon know," Papa remarked.

Two uniformed Maine state police officers and an angry-looking man in a business suit stepped out of a boat onto Papa's dock two days after the family council had discussed Mr. Sampson and his threat that he'd sue to get his grandfather's island back. The man, who seemed to be in charge of the officers, stepped up to a very worried Hannah.

"I'm Detective Eames," he snapped. "Is Harry Parmenter here?"

"I'll get him for you." Hannah motioned toward several chairs on the porch as she raced upstairs to find Papa, who was busy helping Mama wallpaper a room in preparation for the fall tourist season.

The policemen had not taken seats when Hannah returned with Papa. Hannah waited beside Papa, who put his arm across her shoulders as if to say, Stick around, Hannah. You're in this, too, and you need to hear the rest of it.

"Sampson's clean, Mr. Parmenter," began Detective Eames, in a voice that made Hannah think he'd eaten unripe lemons for breakfast. "No drugs. And no marijuana growing under lights in his attic. The blue light your kids saw is his TV—he sometimes watches all night."

"Well, I guess he's entitled to do that," Papa said.

"Sam Sampson's not a tidy housekeeper, exactly, what with keeping his pigs downstairs while he sleeps upstairs," the detective added.

"Those miniature potbellies make great house pets, I've heard," Papa chuckled, trying to lighten things up for three very embarrassed law enforcement officers. "However, I told you on the phone exactly what I knew to be true. *You* chose to get the search warrant, detective. Now *I've* got an angry neighbor to live with."

"And incidently, Miss Parmenter, I need your full name, date of birth, and Social Security number before I leave," the detective added.

"Why do you need that information?" Papa protested.

"Mr. Sampson plans to appear at the courthouse tomorrow and swear out a warrant for Miss Parmenter's arrest on charges of assault with a deadly weapon. He claims your daughter threatened him with a shotgun."

"I didn't threaten him," Hannah said, sounding scared.

Papa hugged Hannah more tightly.

"Well," the detective added, softening his tone, "I doubt that you have anything to worry about. I expect the judge'll ask you a few questions and dismiss the case. You might want to retain an attorney, though."

"Can...can Sam Sampson sue you?" Hannah fretted as soon as the officers left. Worried as she was that she'd be fined, even jailed as a criminal, Hannah was far more sorry she'd gotten Papa into trouble—though she knew it was not really all her fault.

"He can't sue us over the drug search, honey. That was a police decision to act without further evidence."

"Maybe we should try to make friends with our...our new neighbor."

"I think you're right, but it's not going to be easy now," Papa checked his watch. "Got t' get back upstairs. Mama's waiting with that wallpaper."

Hannah held Hunter's head on her knee for a long, long time as she sat on the porch steps that afternoon. "Ol' hound, you 'n I've got a lot to learn," she murmured at last.

"Dear Jesus," Hannah prayed, "forgive me for taking things into my own hands.

Chapter Eight

The Electric Pirate

"I'd like you to help Walter clean out the spring this morning, Hannah." Papa didn't often ask Hannah to do outdoor work beyond her regular chores of taking turns with Walt at feeding the chickens and milking Molly, their family cow. But Papa was tied up for several days helping Mama hang wallpaper in upstairs bedrooms that needed redecorating before the fall tourist season began. And cleaning the spring on the side of Bald Hill, which was Beaver Lodge's water supply, was a job that needed two people.

"Sure, Papa. Be glad to help Walt." To tell the truth, getting out of the house and raising a sweat from hard work sounded good to Hannah, since it might help her to get her mind off her troubles. She'd really messed things up by taking matters into her own hands trying to solve the mystery of the pigs and the blue light.

Only yesterday the sheriff had arrived with a subpoena for Hannah's court appearance on a criminal charge of assault with a deadly weapon.

"I'd rather deliver these papers to y' neighbor," the sheriff had indignantly remarked when he handed Hannah the subpoena and explained the importance of the papers to her.

"It's an easier trip up to the spring since Papa and I put in that new electric pump," Walt remarked a few minutes later as he and Hannah trudged uphill toward the pump house. Lugging a heavy ladder from the barn, Walt plodded along behind Hannah, who carried a shovel, two plastic buckets, and a length of nylon rope.

"Sure is," Hannah agreed glumly. She peered up the hillside where Walt had cut a swath through the thicket of young fir trees so that Papa could set poles and string electric wires. Though the old gravity-flow spring had served Beaver Lodge well for many years, a new wing with an upstairs bathroom required a high-pressure water system.

"Now all we need's a water softener," Hannah added sourly.

"Don't take it so hard, Sis."

"You should talk. Your hair's straight as an Indian's, and it's cut short, too. The spring water is so full of minerals that Mama and I have to lug soft water from the lake to get a decent shampoo."

"That court subpoena, I mean," Walt softly answered, aware of what was really eating his sister. "We're all praying for you. Besides, no judge in the state will find you guilty. After the way he talked to you, you couldn't be blamed if you *had* threatened ol' Sampson with my shotgun."

Hannah began to cry quietly. She was at the spring house now, and she unsnapped the latch and scooted inside. The spring was one of Hannah's favorite places. It was always cool in summer, and the gurgle of mountain water quieted her heart and stilled her soul. Often, before Papa had installed a diesel generator to put electric lights and a refrigerator into Beaver Lodge, Hannah had trod up the narrow path in the morning dew to bring home berries, bacon, or milk that Mama had left there to cool.

"Papa says to be sure to shut the pump off before we start to work," Walt cautioned, still panting from lugging the heavy ladder.

"I'll get it, Walt," Hannah chirped, her spirits lifted now. She raised herself on her knees inside the low pump house and gave the big knife switch attached to a metal box on the wall a yank. A heavy wire ran into the box from the pole just outside, and another wire ran out of the box to the pump, which sat beside the shallow well.

"What's this?" Hannah asked, surprised.

"What do you see?" said Walt, who still stood outside trying to figure out the best way to get the long ladder inside and into the well.

"A new wire. It goes out under the wall."

"That's the coaxial cable for our radio telephone's antenna."

As usual, Walt was confident of his superior knowledge of electrical and mechanical things.

"No it's not. Here's the coaxial cable over here by itself. It's round, like on Aunt Theresa's cable TV. I *know* what a coaxial cable looks like. But this new cable is kinda flat, like the wires the electrician ran in the lodge's new wing."

"Let me have a gander." Walt flopped onto his back. Grabbing the low doorway, he pulled himself inside the low building, a little larger than a doghouse.

"Well, I'll be a monkey's uncle!" Walt exclaimed, crouching next to Hannah. "Papa hasn't said anything about putting up a new outdoor light."

"Let me out, Walt!"

"Sure." Walt doubled up and rolled out, and Hannah crawled outside behind him. She began to kick at the leaves and dirt on the uphill side of the pump house.

"Gimme that shovel."

Walt passed her the shovel.

"See here. I 'most cut it right in two." Hannah's first shovelful of dirt left the new wire bare, for not more than three inches of earth and leaves hid it from sight.

"Wow!" said Walt. "Whoever buried that electric wire was in a hurry. And look there!" He pointed up the steep hillside. Here and there, where gaps in the thin mountainside foliage showed bare ground, a faint, but obvious line in the dirt showed where someone had dug a shallow ditch, then covered it up.

"Let's follow it, Walt." Before Walt could answer, Hannah was scrambling up the front of Bald Hill, using the tree branches and outcroppings of rock for handholds.

Brother and sister were panting when they reached the edge of the blueberry barren. Without stopping to catch their breath, they followed the freshly buried wire along the edge of the field. The covered-up ditch went as far as the oak tree, where Hannah had first seen the herd of Vietnamese pigs.

Here the wire was hidden by the stone wall that separated the Parmenter property from the old Sampson place. It ran on top of the ground, out of sight from the blueberry field but in plain sight of anybody who crossed the old stone wall.

"I'm going to follow this a ways—see where it goes," Walt said.

"Walt, please."

"Please what?"

"We can *see* that it goes downhill, toward the Sampson house."

Hannah was as angry as Walt with Mr. Sampson because it now seemed certain that their new neighbor was stealing electricity. But her encounter with Sam Sampson had already brought shame on Papa and had landed her in court, Hannah considered. *"Please* be careful!"

"Phooey! He's neither armed nor dangerous. His talk's nuthin' but hot air."

Walt disappeared down the pig trail among a grove of young pines while Hannah hunkered against the wall, waiting and praying. In ten minutes by Hannah's watch—though it seemed like hours—her brother was back.

"Well, is he a thief?"

"Yup. Wire goes right through a window in that old house."

"Let's get on home."

"Agreed," laughed Walt. "Guess our new friend won't be watching any TV for a while! Wait'll we tell Papa!"

Papa agreed with Walt that Mr. Sampson indeed would *not* watch any more free TV. With Walt's help, Papa disconnected Sampson's cable, then he pulled perhaps fifty feet of it out of the shallow ditch, cutting it with pliers. Hannah coiled the wire, then carried it to Papa's tool shed to hang on a nail.

"Are you going to have Mr. Sampson arrested for stealing our electricity, Harry?" Mama asked at suppertime. Although she felt that their neighbor deserved to be arrested, she also feared that Sam Sampson would make trouble if Papa called the law.

"I think I'll let him stew in his own juice for a week or so," Papa answered thoughtfully.

"What do you mean, Papa?" inquired Hannah.

"Just this: I suspect our neighbor believes we *owe* him something. Sooner or later he'll find a way to let us know just what it is he wants."

"Like beaver trapping rights on Juniper Bog?" Walt wondered.

"That—and a lot more, probably."

One week after Papa disconnected Sam Sampson's illegal wire, a strange motorboat pulled up to Papa's pier and a young man got out. Hannah thought the fellow seemed nervous when he introduced himself as "the legal aide to Mr. Edmond S. Ashcroft, III, attorney at law." The young man passed Papa a sheaf of papers.

"What's all this?" Papa inquired.

"Mr. Ashcroft has been retained by Mr. Samuel H. Sampson in the matter of Sampson versus Parmenter et al.," the aide answered stiffly. "Sign here please, mister."

"Sign here please, *sir*," corrected Mama, who had listened, her indignation growing hotter by the moment.

"Uh, sir," the young man corrected himself. Papa signed.

"You might have offered the poor fellow a doughnut and a cup of coffee, Sandy," Papa said, chuckling as he watched lawyer Ashcroft's aide get into his motorboat. "I do appreciate your sticking up for my dignity, though," he added thoughtfully, kissing Mama, who was crying hot tears of anger by now.

"Papa, why didn't you tell that guy off?" Hannah asked later that evening. "Sam Sampson is nothing but a...an electric *pirate!*"

Papa looked up from reading his Bible. "I could have. Most folks would think it was justified. But I'm not sure that's what Jesus would have us do. The man was just doing his job."

"But you...you laughed?"

"I wasn't laughing at him, Hannah. I was laughing at my *own* predicament. 'A merry heart does good like medicine,' wise King Solomon said. And another thing," Papa held up the sealed sheaf of court papers, "I'm not even going to open these until tomorrow morning. Then I'll be rested and able to make wiser decisions."

"I think," Hannah added, smiling thoughtfully, "sometimes we're wise to wait upon the LORD, 'stead o' always trying to solve all our problems at once."

Chapter Nine

Who's the Thief?

"I guess," said Papa at breakfast, "when Hannah called Mr. Sampson a pirate, she was right on the money."

Papa had been up since before dawn with his Bible and the legal papers. He had been asking the Lord for direction, but it still seemed like Sam Sampson was trying to rob them.

"What are we going to *do*, Harry?" fretted Mama. "He demands that you give him Beaver Island—all except the corner where we've got the lodge—and pay him thousands of dollars for that timber you sold off land he says still belongs to his family. We *can't* repay that. We used it all to pay off our mortgage."

"And he says he'll have you persecuted for timber theft if you don't pay him," Walt added, sounding as concerned as Mama.

"You mean prosecuted, Walt," corrected Hannah. Until now Hannah had not uttered a single word this morning. The worse things began to sound, the more confidence God seemed to give her. Today, like

Papa, Hannah was not even concerned about her upcoming trial for criminal assault.

"One thing at a time," Papa said slowly. "First, the claims of criminal prosecution for timber theft are an empty threat. Sampson probably knows that. He knows very well that his grandfather sold both the timber lot and the lodge to the men who developed Beaver Lodge, except his house and forty acres. Bald Hill was purchased later to give the lodge a better water supply than a lake polluted by hundreds of cottages. He's got to prove in court that I intended to steal from him. I know that there was no theft, and I think he knows it."

"Yuck," said Hannah, who had shampooed in lake water that very morning.

"And we have copies of all three of the deeds," Papa concluded.

"Then the whole lawsuit's a fraud!" Mama exclaimed. "The man *is* a pirate. I'm going over there myself this very morning!"

"There's just one problem," Papa said, tapping the legal documents. "Lawyer Ashcroft asserts that there are no deeds of record to show that old Adam Sampson ever sold Beaver Island, except for this small corner. And he's done a little searching at the courthouse in Foxcroft to prove it."

"What does that mean, Papa?" Hannah wondered.

"It means that the deeds to our property, which I have photocopies of, were never recorded."

"Then our deeds are worthless!" Mama blanched white.

"No, Sandy," Papa said patiently. "An unrecorded deed in this state is every bit as valid as a recorded one. But we'll need to find the originals to prove it."

"But the lawyers?" Mama's color was coming back.

"It's the lawyers who are the key to unraveling this..."

"This mystery," Hannah completed Papa's thought.

"Lawyers know what's legal and what isn't legal. If we can prove to Sam Sampson's lawyer that our papers are legal, they'll drop the case—even if Sampson wishes to continue—because they know that the judge will throw the case out of court. And we need also to find the lawyer who drew up the deeds when old Adam Sampson sold Beaver Island to the investors thirty years ago. But the next step is a head-to-head chat with young Mr. Sampson," Papa chuckled.

Mama was aghast. "You...you're supposed to fight him in *court!*"

"The best agreements are made *out* of court," Papa said. "But I'll need a witness. Who wants to come along?"

"I'll go," said Mama. "The kids can finish the housework."

"What will you do if Sampson gets ugly—swears at us, maybe?" Papa asked.

"I'd give him a piece of my mind," Mama said stoutly.

"Would that help?"

"I suppose not. But it *would* make me feel better."

Everyone around the table, Mama included, laughed.

"Ruff, r-r-r-ruff, ruff!" Hunter, who had been sleeping in front of the wood-burning stove, chimed in.

"You would rather stay home, wouldn't you, Sandy?" Papa asked.

"Yes," Mama admitted. Her zeal to scold Sam Sampson had cooled as quickly as it had arisen.

"Don't look at me," said Walt. He had been brave enough the day he and Hannah had found the illegal wire. But the thought of meeting Mr. Sampson made him nervous.

"I'll go," Hannah quietly volunteered. "I'd like to meet our neighbor on more..." she searched for a word, "on more congenial terms."

"Are you sure?"

"Very sure, Papa."

"Well then," said Papa, "before we go we need to ask the Lord's direction and blessing."

"I'll pray," offered Mama, who still wanted some part in dealing with their angry neighbor.

" 'When a man's ways please the Lord, he makes his enemies to be at peace with him,' " Mama quoted from Proverbs as she prayed. "Father, You know how we wish to be honest and honor You," Mama prayed. "Mr. Sampson thinks we're dishonest, and he has decided to be our enemy. But please honor your promise. Give us peace with our new neighbor. In Jesus' name, Amen."

Hannah's knees began to shake even before Papa beached the motorboat at Sampson Cove. Her heart bravely wanted to be there. But she was scared, all the same. "Suppose he's got a gun, Papa?"

"Did he have a gun when you met him in the woods?"

"Well, no."

"Then don't worry about it. He's a bully, and bullies are cowards. They use lawyers and the police to intimidate honest people. And, oh—I have a confession to make."

"What's that, Papa?"

Papa glanced toward the steps leading up

through the underbrush to the Sampson house. "I'm a coward sometimes, too. If I'd simply come over here and chatted with...with our new neighbor when you and Walter told us about that blue light in the attic window instead of phoning the Maine State Police, things might have been much different. Solomon wisely said that 'a soft answer turns away wrath.' I should have remembered that," Papa added.

"At least then he couldn't hold the drug search against us," Hannah agreed.

"You guys carrying any guns?" Sam Sampson peered suspiciously past his front door. The rank odor of pigs that wafted out made Hannah hope that they did not get invited inside.

"No, sir!" Papa replied. "Just coming to pay a neighborly visit. Something we ought to have done weeks ago."

"Well, you ain't welcome," Sampson replied, swearing.

"I didn't ask to be welcome," Papa said. No trace of anger showed in his voice. "There are things we both need to discuss—for the benefit of both of us. First, I'm here to apologize. I had no business calling the cops on you. I wouldn't want you to treat me like that."

"And I didn't mean to point a shotgun at you," Hannah said, peeking around Papa's coat sleeve.

"Well, well, ain't we the humble ones. Nobody apologizes, 'less they've got something up their sleeve. As fer you, missy, apology accepted."

"Does that mean I'm not...not arrested any-more?" Hannah was uncertain just how to word the question.

Sam shrugged. "No hard feelin's. I can drop *them* charges. I got a little girl m'self." He squinted at Papa. "Your case is different. You stole my land, and I expect to be paid for my timber you illegally appropriated."

"Exactly when did I steal your land, sir? I bought the lodge from the investors who bought out your grandfather. They furnished me copies of warrantee deeds with the signatures of Adam Sampson or his son for all three parcels of land. I can show you if you like."

"My attorney says there ain't no deeds of record conveying nuthin' but the ten acres with your lodge, barn, an' pasture. Now, I ain't even s'pose to be talkin' t' you outside o' the courthouse."

"Try to put yourself in my spot for a moment. You've spent thousands of dollars to establish a business, then you're told your deeds are fakes. You'd want to talk to the other guy and try to learn exactly what's going on."

"And I'm the other guy, right?"

"That's right, Sam—may I call you Sam? I'm Harry."

"And I'm Hannah," interrupted Hannah.

"Well, you've got the papers from my attorney by now, I expect."

"I expect there are things you really want that aren't mentioned in the lawsuit. You need electricity, for instance."

"You goin' t' have me arrested f' stealin' y' juice?"

"That's a felony, if I were to pursue it," Papa said firmly. "But I could overlook that. You need to run a water pump if you're going to keep pigs. My generator is big enough for both of us, probably. I might *sell* you the electricity."

"What about my missing pigs—the ones your dog killed. I found three dead."

"How many in all?" asked Papa.

"Eight—ten, mebbe."

Hannah caught her breath. She knew there were probably fifteen, besides the three Mr. Sampson had found dead.

"What are they worth?"

"Fifty bucks apiece. Them's top quality potbellied pigs. I plan to sell them to pet stores."

"$500 about right, then?" Papa asked affably. "We can probably manage that, if you can justify it. But are *you* willing to concede anything?"

"Yeah. But I gotta have free electricity for three years—I figger it'll take me that long to get my pig farm established. I can drop the timber theft charges. But I'll insist on Grandpa Sampson's land back—every acre of it."

"Tell you what," Papa said, his eyes a-twinkle. "Can we say we've agreed to come to terms? We just won't try to nail anything down until we've both had time to think more about it."

"And pray about it," Hannah said under her breath.

"Yeah," agreed Mr. Sampson.

"These legal matters take time," Papa added. "The court date is two months away. But I'd guess you'd rather not wait that long before we hook your electricity back up. Meantime, I'll see if I can find the original copies of those deeds and receipts signed by Adam Sampson when he sold the land. Your attorney will want to see them. And by the way," Papa added, "as soon as we work things out, I'll be happy to talk about *selling* some electricity."

"Shore. You won't find nuthin' new, though."

"And say," said Papa, "my wife Sandy runs our hotel dining room at Beaver Lodge with the help of Hannah, here. We do serve meals. First one's on the house. My wife makes a wicked good raspberry pie," Papa chuckled, using a well-known Maine expression to describe what he believed to be the best pie north of Boston. "You're welcome anytime. Stop over next week, and we'll compare papers. Maybe we can both save some legal fees and court time."

Papa offered his hand to Mr. Sampson. To Hannah's complete surprise, Sam shook Papa's hand.

Sam's Family

"How did it go at the courthouse in Foxcroft today?" Mama's question was directed at whoever was more ready to talk—Papa or Hannah.

"Strange," said Papa.

"We met some strange people, too," Hannah chirped.

"Strange? Strange people?" Mama inquired.

"Strange business," said Papa, "like a lawyer who left a drawer full of unfinished paperwork when he retired. Six months later he took sick, and his business was left unfinished—for more than twenty years."

"Now *you're* getting mysterious. May I assume that the unfinished business involves us? Though I don't see how it could. We didn't own Beaver Lodge twenty years ago, and we weren't even married yet." Mama was puzzled. "And strange people?"

"Strange, as in Sampson strange," Hannah continued.

"More Sampson heirs? Do *they* want to sue us, too?"

"Not heirs, fortunately," Papa said. "Sam Sampson has a wife and two kids, and we can probably expect them here tomorrow," Papa sighed. "Sam's been using the old Sampson place to hide out from his wife."

"Are they divorced? Coming here?" Mama was startled.

"Not divorced," said Papa.

"They *are* coming here," Hannah said. "I sort of invited them—with Papa's permission, of course."

"Sort of?" Mama was now puzzled.

"Mama, it was either here, or they'd have to live with the pigs."

"Well, *I'm* going over there this very afternoon and clean house for Mr. Samuel H. Sampson!" said Mama. "They *can't* stay here long—we've got fall tourists coming soon. Mr. Sampson had better help or stay out of my way! But how on earth did you get hooked up with *them?*"

"Mrs. Sampson is from New Hampshire, and it seems that when Sam disappeared, she had a pretty good idea he'd gone to northern Maine, 'cause he'd bragged about owning some property up here," Papa explained. "She packed her kids into an old rattletrap station wagon and drove to Foxcroft to see what she could find out. She and I were looking for the same property records when we met," Papa explained.

"But he's been on this island before!" Mama exclaimed. "She must have known that."

"He sure has, Mama. Beaver trapping," Hannah agreed.

"Evidently he did his disappearing act then, too," Papa said wryly. "He can't seem to decide whether he wants to stay with his family or come to the Maine wilderness and live like a hermit."

"Hermit, schmermit! I'll teach him some responsibility on the end of a broom!" Mama was indignant. "Did you tell Mrs. Sampson where to find her pig-farmer husband?"

"Well, she did ask for directions. But she had most of it figured out herself from the records on the family deeds," Papa said helplessly. "She and their kids are stranded in Foxcroft with only money for tonight's motel bill and not gas enough to get back to New Hampshire. We couldn't just turn them away."

"So!" Mama glared at Papa, then she hugged him. "You know," she said, "someone in this family needs to have a soft heart. I wouldn't have you any other way. We'll *all* welcome the Sampsons tomorrow. But today I'm going to give *Mr.* Sam a lesson in wife and child care." Mama sighed. "Did you learn anything about our deed to Beaver Lodge?" she asked finally.

"Yes," Papa grinned. "And we're not even going to have to pay a lawyer. It seems that the attorneys for the men who built Beaver Lodge had a senior partner die with some business unfinished about twenty years ago. Since it was their mistake, they've agreed to file the proper papers and deal with Sam Sampson's lawyer for us free. They expect all charges against me will be dropped, once Sam's lawyer sees the papers. They had our deeds in their files!"

"Oh, Harry!" Mama squealed. She hugged Papa harder, crying. "When Jesus said, 'Give and it shall be given unto you,' I suspect He may have had times like this in mind. You gave kindness to Mrs. Sampson and her children, Harry. And the Lord gave us a clear title to Beaver Lodge without the expense and bother of a court lawsuit."

Hannah listened in glad wonder as Mama spoke. How proud she was of Papa. How glad Hannah was that God had touched Mama's heart with a desire to help the Sampsons, too.

"Hannah," Mama said finally, "I'm going to need some help from you. Please get our cleaning equipment together."

"Yes, Mama. An' I think we're going to need a shovel, too."

Hannah *did* need the shovel, but as Mama put it later, "Sam hadn't let the pigs quite as far into the house as it seemed by the smell outside the front door." The pigs were, in fact, confined to the woodshed, a large room next to the kitchen. Sam kept them out of his living quarters by a gate that let the odors in and let him toss them scraps without having to open a door.

"I told him he'd either get the pigs out of the house *all the way* or I'd call the health department," Mama chuckled. "There's enough of his grandfather's old barn left to make a pretty good pigsty until he can buy lumber to build a new one."

"The flies were *dreadful*," Hannah put in.

"How did he take it when you told him his wife and kids are coming tomorrow?" Papa inquired.

"I've never seen a man so crushed," Mama said. "He sat and cried. I was ashamed of myself for being angry at him when I went over there. It's going to take all the help we can give him to rebuild his family. I'm convinced that his attack on us was a cry for help."

Mama's eyes shined with a new purpose. Ever since Papa and Hannah had told her that Sam Sampson's family was coming to Beaver Island, she had worried about what she should do. Now she knew! On the way home from the Sampson house, a verse she and Hannah had read together just last week took on new meaning, and she excitedly realized what the verse really meant when it said if your enemy hungers, feed him and if he thirsts give him drink. Sam Sampson had been their enemy by threatening to take away their home, and now they could help him!

"Can . . . can I help?" Walt had been listening all the while, amazed at his mother's changed attitude toward Sam Sampson.

"I expect you can," Papa agreed. "Why don't you offer to help him build some pens for those pigs? And be sure any tools you take over there come back with you the same day. Sam may need to borrow them again sometime," Papa advised. "I can't loan them to him again if he loses 'em." For once, Papa was the practical one.

It was nearly noon the next day when the phone rang. Hannah took the call, and she discovered it was Mrs. Sampson calling from Uncle Joe and Aunt Theresa Boudreau's in Laketon. Papa had told her to phone from there when she got to Laketon. Hannah passed Mama the phone.

"Yes, we'd love to have you," Mama said. "We have lots of room—Beaver Lodge is a tourist home, you know." Mama listened for a moment. "It's on us," she said. "We're nearly empty until hunting season starts, so you won't be taking up any rented room space. *We* know what it's like to be up against the wall with no place to turn—the Lord has seen us through, and He'll meet your needs, too. No...no, I can't let you move in with Sam until we get some more cleaning done."

Mama put the phone down. "Hannah, is there a motorboat ready?"

"I'll go gas one up, Mama. Want me to go to Laketon for the Sampsons?"

"Yes. On second thought, no. I'll go myself. Mrs. Sampson's got an old station wagon full o' baggage, besides two kids. We'll have to store most of it in the Boudreau's garage for a few days, and I'll need to help her decide what to bring to Beaver Lodge."

✿ ✿ ✿ ✿ ✿ ✿ ✿

"I'll do them dishes," Mrs. Sampson insisted. "You bin good enough, takin' us in like this."

"You're our guest, Judith," protested Mama. "Besides, Hannah and I are used to a houseful of guests."

"You cooked. I'll wash," rasped Sam's wife. "An' I got plenty o' help. Melanie, here, she kin do a woman's work ennytime. C'mon Mell," her mother screeched. "Git them plates t' the sink."

Eight-year-old Melanie meekly obeyed.

"Mama!" It was Paul, Sam and Judith's Sampson's five-year-old. "Wipe my nose."

To the perfect astonishment of the Parmenters, Mrs. Sampson wiped her son's runny nose on the dirty tail of her own shirt. "Now you run outside an' play," she commanded, swearing. "Excuse my French," she added, smiling weakly at Mama.

Mama was about to insist that Mrs. Sampson leave the kitchen when Papa interrupted. "I need some help in the barn, Sandy," he said mildly. "Can you come out with me?"

Hannah and Walt knew it was very unusual for Papa to ask Mama, who had the responsibility of running the kitchen of a small hotel, to traipse after him to the barn. Sensing that he had something else in mind, they, with Mama, grabbed their jackets and followed Papa to the barn.

"That woman is going to be a handful to deal with, Sandy," Papa said, as soon as they were out of Mrs. Sampson's hearing.

"And she *swore* at little Paul." Walt was shocked.

"Speaking of little Paul." Hannah turned toward the young boy, who had followed the family into the barn. He was a beautiful child, flaxen-haired, with expressive blue eyes. Round cheeks proved that whatever hardships the Sampson family had suffered, hunger was not one of them. Hannah hugged Paul, picking him up.

"Lemme down!" cried the frightened child. The curiosity that had brought him to the barn was not great enough to enable him to overcome his fear of strangers. Paul kicked Hannah so hard with his muddy sneakers that she dropped him at once.

"I'll take him," said Walt, realizing that Papa had things to say not meant for Paul's ears. "C'mon, Paul, let's go see the motorboat."

"Sandy, I'm sorry. I've loaded you down with a bit of a burden, I'm afraid."

"You don't need to be, Harry." Mama took Papa's arm. "We haven't been able to do much in church because we're so tied down with our work here. God's sent me someone to minister to right here at home, that's all."

"I'll help, Mama," Hannah offered. "I can entertain Mell. Maybe even make friends with Paul."

"I know you will, darling. And I think," Mama continued, "that Judith is just wound up today! She's overtired, embarrassed at being helped by strangers, maybe even a little fearful of what the future holds for her and her children."

"And she likes to take charge—to run things," Papa observed.

"I can see that plain enough," "Mama chuckled. "Once she rests overnight I may put her in charge of getting a house ready for her family—after we chase Sam outside with his pigs!"

Chapter Eleven

Hannah, Hannah Raise a Pig!

"This is the third time in a week Walt has had to go to Laketon with one of our boats to rescue Sam Sampson," Papa observed one fall evening at suppertime. "There are plenty of used boat motors for sale cheap this time of year," Papa added.

"Then why doesn't Mr. Sampson just buy one?" Hannah wanted to know.

"Even a hundred dollars for a used outboard motor is a dear price if you don't have it," Mama observed. "Sam had to use the hundred dollars he got from selling his wife's old station wagon to put tires on his truck, Judith told me only yesterday. And he needs his pickup truck to haul his fancy pigs to market."

"I guess you're right," Hannah agreed, remembering when the Parmenter family had found $100 or even $10 hard to come by. "But getting the pigs to Laketon in his boat *is* part of hauling to market. And if those oriental pigs are worth as much as fifteen thousand dollars apiece as fancy house pets, like Marie said in her letter, then he ought to afford a *new* boat."

"Sam Sampson is raising culls—runts, that he gets cheap from that farm in Foxcroft," said Papa, who had learned a bit about their neighbor's business now that Sam Sampson realized that Papa and the rest of the Parmenter family really wished to be his friends. "Those are worth fifty dollars apiece at most, many a lot less." Papa rubbed his chin. "Hannah, how many of Sam's pigs did Hunter eat?"

"Fifteen, Papa."

"Well,...." Papa sighed and continued. "I paid him fifty dollars apiece for the ten he said were missing, but I guess that money was spent on groceries and other necessities soon after Judith arrived with the kids."

"You don't owe Sam another cent!" said Mama, concerned that Papa was getting a soft heart just when the Parmenter family was short of money, too. "Those pigs were all on *our* land when Hunter caught them. And after the trouble Sam caused us, you ought to have *him* prosecuted for stealing electricity!"

"The Lord's been too good to us to treat our neighbor like that, Sandy," Papa answered thoughtfully.

The early eastern evening had fallen over the Maine wilderness by the time Walt returned from Laketon with Sam Sampson—and a new load of piglets from the Foxcroft fancy Vietnamese pig farmer. Walt stopped at Beaver Lodge to borrow Papa's gas lantern before puttering over to Sampson Cove to help unload the baby potbellied porkers.

"Evening, Mrs. Parmenter," said Sam, who had come with Walt into the lodge. "*Cold,* ridin' 'crost the lake this time o' year. Hi, Harry" he added, as Papa, who had just carried some guests' luggage upstairs, entered the kitchen. "I got me a fine load o' potbellies this time—twenty of 'em."

"Hello, Sam," Mama, who was working at the stove, cooly greeted their neighbor. Mama tried to be friendly, but she hadn't really gotten over Sam's unpleasant entrance to Beaver Island. "What are you going to do with twenty babies?" she asked politely. "Don't they need an incubator until they get a little size on 'em?"

"No bigger'n rats, Mama," Walter put in.

"Oh, I'll incubate them all right. I've built me a big box out o' old boards from that tumbledown barn. I'm keeping them in the kitchen by the stove until they're ready to go outside with the others."

Mama, who was cooking up a batch of soup stock for the guests at Beaver Lodge, at once began to stir vigorously, and she did not answer.

"Baby pigs don't smell at the very first, if you change the papers every day," said Papa. He had sensed that Mama was upset at Sam's plan to put pigs, even babies, in the house with his family.

"Not much, anyways," said Sam, who went outside with Walt into the dark with Papa's lantern.

"Who was that?" Hannah came into the kitchen in her bathrobe, her hair in rollers, when she heard the door slam.

"Hannah, we have guests in the house!" Mama scolded.

"I used the *back* stairs," Hannah said, rolling her eyes up in mock disgust. Mama had said nothing about Hannah's going about in a corduroy robe, even last summer. Maybe having neighbors was getting to her.

"That was Sam and Walt. They've got a batch of baby Vietnamese potbellies," Papa at last answered Hannah's question, ignoring her irritation at being corrected. "Stopped to borrow my lantern so they wouldn't have to unload them at the cove in the dark."

"Tempting for hungry owls," said Mama.

"O-o-o-o-o-o-o-oh!" squealed Hannah, remembering that she had once encountered a pig-hungry great horned owl at Sampson Cove.

"O-o-o-o-o-o-o-o-oh," mimicked Hunter, who was sleeping on a braided rug beside the wood-fired kitchen range.

"I'll bet they're darling. I've got to go see them tomorrow."

"Tomorrow is Sunday," Mama reminded Hannah. "The guests will leave when we leave for Sunday school. We'll spend the afternoon with Uncle Joe and Aunt Theresa so we can go to the evening service. Is your Sunday school lesson ready?"

"Part. I'll go up and finish it right away." Hannah grabbed a cookie from the crockeryware cookie goose on the kitchen counter. Then she poured a cold glass of Molly's rich Jersey milk from the refrigerator.

✳ ✳ ✳ ✳ ✳ ✳ ✳

"Those piglets are the last straw!"

Hannah stood late Monday forenoon in the front kitchen door of the Sampson house watching helplessly as Judith Sampson cursed and raved at Sam about having twenty grunting, squealing miniature Vietnamese pigs in the kitchen. Sam had built a box, all right. It was bigger than the kitchen table, and it sat in front of Judith's hot wood-burning stove. Hannah understood the problem, for the kitchen was the only warm place in the Sampson house, and the baby pigs had to have heat.

"Why can't you cut the box in *half?* Push it over there!" Judith swore again, and she gave the box a vicious kick, which sent the terrified piglets rushing to one corner of their wooden nursery.

Sam cursed under his breath, then bent over his box of pigs, gently unpiling them.

"They'll smother to death if they pile up like this," Sam told his wife.

Hannah could see that Mrs. Sampson was right about the box. Cut it in half, and it would fit in a corner, out of the way. But in a week or two, Hannah realized, the pigs would outgrow such a small box. Baby pigs, even miniature ones, grow at an extraordinary rate.

Judith Sampson must have read Hannah's mind, for she now turned to her. "Half a box and half the number of pigs!" she shouted. "You want t' take ten of 'em home, Hannah?"

"My...my mother would never permit them in the kitchen," Hannah stammered.

"See. What'd I tell you?" Judith bored into Sam, her eyes blazing. "Parmenters won't have 'em stinkin' up their house, either!"

It occurred just then to Hannah that Mrs. Sampson was being terribly unfair to Sam. He seemed to be trying hard to make a living for his wife and children under very tough circumstances. After all, there weren't that many ways to earn a living on Beaver Island. On the other hand, it certainly wasn't right for Sam to expect his wife to share her kitchen with twenty baby pigs, Hannah knew.

"Perhaps we *could* put some of them in our hen-house," Hannah gently suggested. "Papa's killed the hens and put 'em all in our freezer, and he says we're not getting any new chickens until spring."

A smaller pig box would fit nicely into the corner of the Sampson kitchen, out of the way, Hannah could see. If Judith Sampson were really willing to go along with that, Hannah had helped the Sampsons work out a happy compromise.

※ ※ ※ ※ ※ ※ ※

"If you bring any of those baby pigs over to keep in our henhouse, just be sure you know in advance what your share is when they're sold," Mama warned Hannah that evening.

"Sam's already agreed to give me half the sale price," said Hannah, her eyes shining happily.

"Those pigs aren't going to run the Sampsons out of their home in the next couple of days," Papa put in thoughtfully. "Meanwhile, you need to use a very sharp pencil and your calculator to figure exactly what it's going to cost you to keep them. Ask Sam how much feed he gives his pigs week by week as they grow. Call the feed store in Laketon and get some feed prices. Don't jump in until you've sounded the depth of the water," Papa added.

Hannah had had plenty of experience in jumping in since her family had moved to Moosehead Lake. Some of this jumping in had been before she really knew how deep the water was, so she knew what Papa meant. She remembered that when she and Walt had tried to make money salvaging the wreck of the *President Lincoln*, except for the unusual finds of dolls and chinaware, they had taken only enough treasure to pay for their diving equipment.

"I'll start by measuring the henhouse first thing tomorrow morning. I need to know what it's going to cost me to heat it until the pigs can keep themselves warm. May I use the kerosene brooder stove you use with baby chicks, Papa?"

"I don't know why not," Papa agreed. "You can figure it'll use about two gallons of fuel a day, at a dollar fifteen a gallon. Remember, though, that pigs, like all livestock, will eat more food as it gets colder. I have charts in my file drawer of farm records you'll need to consult if you're going to do this scientifically," Papa advised.

"Aren't they *too* darling for words, Mama?" Hannah and Mama stood shin-deep in loose straw a day later as Hannah's ten Vietnamese potbellied piglets scurried in and out of tunnels they had made in their bedding in Papa's old henhouse.

Hannah picked up a black-and-white baby pig and handed it to Mama. Then she grabbed a wriggly, rat-sized, all-black fellow and held it close to her sweatshirt, stroking it until it calmed down.

"Why, they're *clean*," Mama said, surprised.

"Papa says they'll stay clean as long as I keep plenty of clean straw and chaff on the floor," Hannah laughed. "He remembered that much from when he was a kid growing up on a farm."

"Well, I'm a city girl, I guess," Mama remarked. "I lived all my life in the city of Skowhegan until we moved to Beaver Island. The only pets we ever had were dogs."

Hannah took Mama's pig from her and put both babies back in the straw together. Then she picked up two more, passing one to Mama.

"You've learned to be awfully *affectionate* with those baby pigs in a short time," Mama said.

"Got to be," Hannah answered in her most businesslike voice. "Sam says we can't sell them as pets unless they're used to being picked up and handled. Nobody wants a wild pig for a house pet. He's tried letting them run in the woods and just giving them attention when they came home at night, but that was a mistake. If I'm gonna raise pigs, I've got to give love to the pigs, as much as pigs can receive love," Hannah added, stroking her pig until it snuggled comfortably against her.

"And more important, we've got to use these pigs as a bridge to love the Sampsons," said Mama. "That reminds me. I plan to bake Mrs. Sampson a fresh apple pie today and take it over there when I go to invite Mell and Paul to Sunday school."

Chapter Twelve

Of Mice and Pigs

"I'll keep you little fellers warm. Never fear, Hannah is near," Hannah sang out. Hannah's shoulders ached that evening as she set two five-gallon pails of hot water into the straw in the henhouse. She watched in satisfaction as five or six tiny Vietnamese piglets crowded around each hot bucket.

"Good boy, Hunter," Hannah giggled, as Hunter, his sleek belly full of meat scraps and dog food, wriggled among the potbellied piggies and let them pretend he was their mother.

September had been colder than usual, and Laketon Amoco Oil & Gas, where Hannah had been buying kerosene for fuel to keep her baby pigs warm, had run out of fuel left over from spring. It would be tomorrow, after Laketon Amoco got its fall supply of kerosene, before Walt could take the boat to Laketon to bring fuel for Hannah's stove. Meanwhile, Hannah must keep her babies from dying from the cold.

Hunter raised his sharp nose and sniffed. Then he stood, causing the big-bellied piglets lying next to him to roll about in the straw.

Suddenly Hunter pounced.

"No!" Hannah shrieked. "No, Hunter!" Hannah knew that Hunter had developed a taste for tender potbellied porkers. But she had been certain he would behave himself when he was well fed and in her presence. So far this cold day Hunter had proved himself a well-mannered nursemaid for the baby pigs, who were out of heat.

Now this. Piglets scurried in all directions as Hannah leaped across the henhouse to seize her hound. But his jaws snapped on a hapless, tiny creature that had tried to scramble out of his reach in the straw. Hunter's nose proved sharper than Hannah's eyes, and he proudly stood, puzzled at his mistress's concern, shaking a wriggling, squealing mouse.

"You rascal! So your nose does know the difference between a rodent and a pig!" Hannah was delighted at this turn of events. And it gave her an idea.

It would be a long, cold night before there would be kerosene for the henhouse stove. Mama offered to let Hannah bring her baby pigs inside Beaver Lodge to spend the night in a box behind the kitchen stove, "so long's you get 'em out of sight to the henhouse before the guests come down for breakfast."

"Hunter and I will spend the night with my babies," Hannah said. She filled two more buckets with hot water at the kitchen sink as she spoke. "I slept in the barn with Hunter the night Molly had her calf—remember?"

Mama did remember. "But you said the pigs' straw is full of *mice!*" Mama shuddered.

Mama had not been afraid of a black bear when they went blueberrying, but mice terrified her. Hannah decided that it would be unkind to point out this inconsistency.

"There are mice in the barn, too—lots of 'em," she said. Hannah had seen Tige, the barn's resident tom, with a mouse many a morning as she milked Molly on Papa's three-legged stool. "We'll be fine, Mama. Hunter the brave will kill the wicked mousies."

"Well, I just hope his hunger for pigs doesn't return," Mama said. Clearly, she had given up the battle to keep Hannah from sleeping with her pigs.

Hannah wore her Bean boots to bed that night in the henhouse straw, fresh from the barn. She carefully tucked the bottoms of her jeans into her boots before lacing them tight. She pulled on a hooded sweatshirt, then wrapped herself in a ratty old quilt. Mama's concern about the mice had made her nervous, and Hannah decided she'd not invite the vermin to crawl inside her clothes.

The piglets found Hannah and Hunter better heaters throughout the night than the kerosene stove had ever been. Hannah found it impossible so much as to roll over without disturbing a warm, wriggly body snuggled under her arm or curled against her back.

And the two mouse tails tail Hannah found laid neatly next to the pigs' waterer when the sun lit the henhouse in the morning told her what Hunter's choice of a midnight snack had been.

Plenty of hot water the next morning, along with the sun's warmth, kept Hannah's babies warm until Walt returned in late forenoon with the kerosene.

And Hannah, willing enough to protect the pigs that which were her investment in income to buy Christmas presents, was personally glad for the small hotel's hot water supply. "I don't know if I've ever enjoyed a shower so much," she said at breakfast.

"How were the mice?" teased Walt.

"Tasty, I'm sure," laughed Hannah. "But you'll need to ask Hunter for the specifics."

"The mice!" Hannah squealed, after she had read the letter from her twin cousins in Boston that Walt had brought with the boatload of supplies from Laketon on the mainland. "They're out of school for a couple of weeks because of a leaky gas main. The city has closed their school while it's being repaired. Can I invite them here, Mama?"

"Squeak, squeak," Walt said, bored. "City cousins!"

"Minnie and Miquie got along very well with you here last time." Mama sounded a little defensive, Walt and Hannah both realized. "You kids need friends your own ages once in a while," Mama admonished.

"They're teenage *girls*, Walt," Hannah teased. Though only a few months older than she, the mice had had their thirteenth birthday since their last visit. Hannah had noticed that her fifteen-year-old brother had begun to find teen girls rather interesting, though he tried to be casual about it around her or their parents.

"They're *cousins*," Walt said sourly. "And females."

❋ ❋ ❋ ❋ ❋ ❋ ❋

"Mice and pigs,
Pigs and mice;
Pigs are great,
But mice are nice"

rhymed Minnie as she sat on the gate just inside the henhouse door with a pig on each arm. Mell Sampson, who had trotted over from the old Sampson place to borrow a cup of sugar for her mother, petted the piglets lovingly as Minnie held them. "Do people *really* buy these creatures for house pets?" Minnie asked.

"Sure do." Hannah straightened up from filling a trough with a mixture of corn mash and milk to fatten up her pigs. "When you get tired of 'em, you've got bacon, ham, and pork chops," she teased.

"We eat 'em at our house," put in Mell, not realizing that Hannah was joking. "Only when the pig's too ugly to sell, though."

"Gross!" exclaimed Miquie. She stopped petting one of the pigs her twin held long enough to shoot a glance of disgust at Hannah. "Eat your *pet?* Once you've learned to love it?"

"I hadn't thought of it that way," Hannah protested mildly. "I'm raising these to sell, so I can't get too attached to them. But I *do* love to hold them," she giggled. Then she added, "C'mon. Let's get back to the house."

Minnie put the piglets back into the straw and slid off the gate to let Hannah swing herself over.

"Good boy, Hunter," Minnie said, happily patting Hunter's head. "You've learned some *manners* since we were here last. He doesn't jump all over you and ruin your clothes like he used to."

"Well, he's not a puppy any longer," Hannah said. "Older dogs don't jump on people. He eats *mice*, though," she teased.

The human mice rolled their eyes at each another and made gagging noises in their throats.

"New boots?" Hannah changed the subject. She pointed at the identical expensive boots on her cousins' feet.

"Yup," Miquie said. "L. L. Bean's best. We got off the bus in Freeport at the L. L. Bean store to shop for a few hours on the way up here yesterday. Greyhound goes right past there every couple of hours, so no prob."

"Nice," Hannah said in genuine appreciation. She had lived in Maine all her life, yet she had never been to her state's most famous store. Her own old Bean boots had been Walt's patched-up ones, which he'd outgrown. Though Hannah was thankful for good footwear, secretly she envied girls whose parents gave them so much freedom that they could just hop off a bus to shop in a strange town.

Then Hannah shot a glance at little Melanie. Guiltily Hannah remembered that Mama had twice asked her to go through her sock drawer and pick out the socks she'd outgrown to give to Mell. The child now wore no socks, and her bare toes stuck out through holes in her old canvas sneakers. "Say, Mell," Hannah called after the girl who was hurrying toward home, "can you come back in about an hour to try on some clothes?"

"Sure can!" Mell skipped happily toward the path past Bald Hill.

"What's this?" Hannah now cried, looking at an unusual animal track right next to her cousins' bootprints.

"Dog tracks," said Minnie. "They're all over the place in your yard."

"Hound tracks, silly," corrected Miquie. "Hannah's pet is a full-blooded Beaver Island hound, Prince *Rex Nobilis* Hunter, III."

"Hound tracks are where people go to watch greyhounds race," said Minnie, not to be outdone by her zany sister mouse. Both girls laughed so hard at their own silly talk that Hannah feared they would go into hysterics.

"Cut it out, mice," Hannah said firmly. "This here's *not* a dog track. Dogs have rounded toes. See there." She pointed to one of Hunter's tracks in the soft earth.

"But what is it?" both girls cried at once.

"It has sharp claws," Hannah noticed. She pointed to the sharp tips of each toe mark. "A raccoon, I think."

"You know more about wild animals than you do about people," said Miquie. "You Jane. Me Tarzan." Both girls again broke into fits of giggles.

Hannah could see that the mice would take some getting used to all over again.

"Where's Miquie?" Hannah asked the next morning. She and Minnie were busy setting breakfast tables for the eight guests who had come to Moosehead Lake to see the fall colors.

"Out in the barn with Walt, I think," Minnie answered, without the usual merry squeak in her voice.

"She likes to watch Molly being milked, I guess," Hannah said pensively. Hannah remembered that when the mice had visited before, Miquie, who had never seen a cow close up, had followed her to the barn where she'd made some unkind, sarcastic remarks about country folks and cows.

Just then Hannah heard the clatter of the kitchen's storm door, and hurried to help Walt with the pail of Molly's milk. The milk needed to be strained through a filter into a stainless steel can, then placed in the big refrigerator in the supply room.

"How does this thing go together?" Miquie asked.

Hannah was surprised to find that the older mouse had beaten her to the big steel milk strainer and had already set it on the counter. Walt, with the milk pail, was just coming in from the barn.

"Let me show you," said Hannah.

Milk strainers aren't all that hard to assemble, and Miquie had most of the parts in place by the time Hannah could cross the kitchen.

Suddenly, "Spr-o-i-n-n-ng!" The large spring-steel ring that held the filter down shot from Miquie's fingers and flew across the room.

Hannah picked it up.

"Let's have it," Miquie squeaked, now realizing that it takes both hands to get it into place.

"Can't yet," Hannah said. "It's been on the floor." She stepped to the sink to wash the ring off as Walt marched past the excited mice and swung the heavy milk pail onto the counter beside the strainer.

"There!" Hannah passed the clean ring to Miquie.

"Lemme have it!" insisted Minnie, who figured it was her turn to try to press the stiff spring-steel ring into the milk strainer.

"'S my job," squeaked Miquie, pushing past Minnie and ramming her arm into the strainer as she stepped onto a low stool to see over the top. "Oops!" she cried, losing her balance.

"Who-o-o-shh!" The bucket of warm, fresh milk turned upside down on the kitchen floor. Three girls and a guy found themselves standing in a pool of milk.

"Oh, my!" It was Mama, coming into the kitchen from the supply room.

Miquie and Minnie both bolted for the hall door.

"Whoa!" Mama commanded, blocking the door. "Look at your feet. We have carpets on our floors." Mama grabbed a roll of paper towels, which she tossed to Hannah. "Outside, all four of you, and rinse off with the garden hose. Then I'd appreciate some help mopping this mess up."

"Hannah, I'm really sorry," Miquie apologized. The mouse sat on the kitchen doorstep yanking off her wet sneakers and wringing out her socks.

"That's all right," Hannah said. "Accidents happen. We haven't used up all of yesterday's milk yet. Good thing Molly's giving a lot of milk this time of year," Hannah added as she squirted the milk off her Bean boots with the garden hose.

"Pigs'll eat kind o' lean for a day or so," Walt observed.

"Yeah?" Miquie wondered.

"I mix the leftover milk with mash to feed my piglets," Hannah explained. "They're sleeker lookin' pigs already than the ones Mr. Sampson is raising."

"To market, to market, to buy a fat pig," Minnie sang. "Yuck," she added, watching warm milk flow from her socks as she wrung them out.

"Here, Walt." Hannah tossed the pistol-grip garden hose at Walter, who waited his turn to rinse his boots off.

Walt missed the catch, and the pistol grip landed handle down. The hose squirted Minnie, who had bent to pick up her sneakers.

"Ee-eek!" shrieked the younger mouse as the cold spring water sprayed her.

Walt dived for the hose, but Minnie yanked it from the middle, so that he only succeeded in stepping on it, this time squirting his cousin full in the face.

But Minnie had the hose now, and she yanked it free of Walt's foot.

Walt laughed. "Last time I saw a wet mouse, it was drowned in a ditch," he chuckled. "Even our cat wouldn't touch it."

"Funny man, huh?" Minnie turned the hose on Walt.

"I think," said Miquie, who was older by a few minutes than her twin, "it's time we adults went inside and helped Aunt Sandy clean up the kitchen floor."

Hannah and Miquie cut a wide circle around Walt and Minnie, who were playing with the hose, then scurried for the front door. "Walt looks like a drowned rat," Hannah laughed as they ducked inside.

"I bet he likes it," Miquie giggled. "I'd squirt him, too, if I had a chance."

Chapter Thirteen

Double Trouble

"Papa says we can use his other boat today," Hannah said one morning. "He and the hotel guests will use the big boat for sightseeing."

The twin cousins had never had a ride on Moosehead Lake except for the short trip from Laketon with Uncle Joe. On their first visit to Beaver Island, the lake had been frozen, and travel was by snowmobile.

"Super!" squeaked the mice in unison.

"Is Walt coming?" Minnie squealed.

Miquie shot her sister a dirty look.

"Papa lets me take the boat only as far as Laketon, or Pond Lily Bay, which is north of our island," Hannah explained, ignoring Minnie's question.

"We'd like to see the *whole* lake," the twins squealed.

"Wait a minute. Do you know how big this lake is?"

"No," admitted Miquie, looking up from where she had been clearing a dining room table. Peering

90

down the lake through the big bay window, she said, "I can see clear to the far end. That's Mt. Kineo down there—right?"

"Right and wrong," laughed Hannah.

"Huh?"

"Moosehead is the largest lake within one state in New England. It's narrow in places, and it bends around Mt. Kineo. The mountain is on a peninsula that only *seems* to be the end of the lake."

"How far is it?" Minnie wondered.

"I've been clear to the end only once," Hannah told her. "It took all morning in Papa's big boat just to get there, and it was dark when we got home."

"*That* far? Well, could we go as far as Mt. Kineo?" Miquie asked.

"Maybe," Hannah hedged. "But only if Walt's along."

"And," said Mama, who had been listening from the kitchen, "if you stay within half a mile of shore, once you get past Laketon."

"We will, Mama," Hannah promised.

"And wear life preservers."

"We will," the mice squeaked. Then they broke into a fit of giggles. "C'mon," said Minnie to Miquie at last, "help me make sandwiches."

That was one thing Hannah liked about the mice. Maybe they *were* just a little crazy, but they always were eager to help, and they never made you wait. Well, almost never.

※ ※ ※ ※ ※ ※ ※

"I get to sit next to Wal-terr!" Minnie sang out, beating her sister to the boat when they left. But after buzzing their way down to Mt. Kineo, the four of them had gone into the Kineo House Hotel for half an hour to visit the gift shop. Miquie had managed to beat Minnie to the seat beside Walt this time, and it looked as though she intended to stay there until they arrived home.

"What's that village over there?" Minnie asked, after they had traveled about halfway home. Clearly, it was not Laketon, for Laketon had a traffic light at the top of the hill.

"That's Laketon Junction," said Hannah.

"Well, I got t' use the bathroom," Minnie responded as soon as Hannah had explained that Laketon Junction is where the old narrow gauge logging railroad through Laketon used to connect with the Canadian Pacific Railway's Quebec-to-Atlantic Ocean line. "That's a store, isn't it? They'd have a bathroom." Minnie pointed toward the old railroad depot, now serving as a store.

"I guess," Hannah shrugged. Let's get on home, she silently complained.

"I need to go real bad," Minnie groaned, acting as though she were in dire distress.

"I'll pull in," agreed Walt. He pointed the boat toward the tiny village's only dock.

Minnie hopped onto the dock before Walt even got the boat stopped. "You guys can wait in the boat. I won't be long."

"I'm comin', too," squeaked Miquie. "I could use a candy bar. Want one, guys?"

"Sure," said Hannah.

"Okay," put in Walt.

Hannah and Walt climbed out of the boat. Candy bars were a rare treat at Beaver Lodge.

To Hannah's surprise, Minnie glared at Miquie, then scurried for the store without another word.

None of the other three needed to use the restroom, so they cruised the aisles looking at stuff while they ate their candy.

"Where's Minnie?" Walt asked after a while. He checked his watch as he finished the last of his three-pack of peanut butter cups.

Miquie was silent.

"I'll go see," said Hannah, when the older mouse did not offer to look for her sister in the bathroom.

Hannah was back in a moment. "No sign of her. You sure she didn't go out the back way?" Hannah pointed toward a red EXIT sign over the storeroom door at the back of the store.

Walt peered out the door. "Nobody near the boat," he announced.

Half an hour spent searching behind every house along the village's only street produced no Minnie.

"I was afraid she'd pull a stunt like this," Miquie sighed at last.

"A stunt like *what?*" Walt demanded.

"Run off."

"You mean as in 'runaway teenager'?"

Hannah had seen a TV news feature one night at Aunt Theresa's about what can happen to girls Minnie's age who run away from home. Through her mind raced a fleeting image of a dead girl, her body dumped in a city alley.

"Has she done this before?" Walt asked.

"Once. Stayed out all night. She came home in the morning by herself."

"Well," said Walt, "let's dope this thing out. There's only two ways to go. North of here the highway peters out into the Allagash Wilderness. If she went south, it goes back to Laketon. Then to Foxcroft—that's the nearest city."

"Think Minnie'd take to the woods?" Hannah looked accusingly at Miquie.

"She's afraid to be in the woods alone. Bears." Miquie shuddered. "And I'm afraid of the woods, too."

"I think we should phone Mama," Hannah said.

"What could Mama do? She's on an island without a boat. Remember? And Papa won't be home until dark."

"Pray, I'm sure," Hannah said.

"We could at least call Uncle Joe. He could drive toward Laketon Junction and maybe find her walking along the road."

Walt fished a quarter out of his pocket. "Good thinking, Sis." He hurried toward the pay phone in the corner of the country store.

But no one was home at Uncle Joe and Aunt Theresa Boudreau's. So Walt dialed 9-1-1.

Hannah and Minnie heard him talking with the police dispatcher. Then Walt, looking concerned, stared at the receiver for a moment before hanging up.

"What's the matter?" Hannah asked.

"The dispatcher at the Maine State Police post just told me there's a hefty fine for filing a false missing person report," Walt said, shaken. Then he punched himself in the head. "I can't believe it!"

"Can't believe what?" Hannah cried.

"I told the police that Minnie Mouse is missing. I forgot our ratty cousin's real name!"

Miquie only giggled.

Walt decided he'd walk down the highway toward Laketon and let Hannah take Miquie back to Beaver Island in the boat. More than an hour later, Hannah and Miquie trudged unhappily up the steps of Beaver Lodge.

Before following Miquie inside, Hannah took a long, last look down the lake. She could see Uncle Joe's house, near the waterfront. Has Walt walked that far yet? she wondered. Hannah knew that Walt knew where their aunt and uncle kept their spare key. So if they still weren't home, he could let himself in and phone the island.

Hannah's eyes followed the row of elms and birches marching northward from Laketon toward Laketon Junction. These, she knew, marked the highway, and here and there she caught the flash of the afternoon sun reflecting off the windshield of a speeding car. Had Minnie hitched a ride in one of these cars? And where is Walt?

Hannah brought her gaze back toward Laketon now. She was surprised to see Uncle Joe's plywood excursion boat, the *President Lincoln II,* paddling away from the mainland.

Hannah charged straight into Mama as she whirled to rush inside with the news.

Mama, who had just heard from Miquie that Minnie had run away, squeezed Hannah tight for a long moment, stifling what Hannah tried to say.

"Mama!" Hannah blurted at last, "Uncle Joe's boat! Minnie and Walt are probably with them!"

"Let's hope they are," said Mama evenly. "I've been praying for them."

Half an hour later, tearful Minnie and a stern Aunt Theresa stepped onto the Beaver Island dock.

"Where's Walter?" Mama asked at once.

"I think," said Aunt Theresa, seeming to ignore Mama's question, "that you twins should go *straight* upstairs to your bedroom. Your Aunt Sandy and I need to talk."

Though it was Mama's place to send the mice to their room, she showed no offense at her childless older sister's intrusion.

"Where *is* Walt?" Mama insisted again, once the twins were out of earshot.

Walt's *my* brother. I guess I've got a right to hear, Hannah told herself, sitting on a porch swing.

"Walt is keeping his Uncle Joe company for a couple of days until his cousins return to Boston," Aunt Theresa said adamantly. "When Walt found Minnie walking along the highway, he refused even to speak with her. He says he thinks she ran off 'cause she's jealous of her older sister getting to be near him more'n she does, and *I* think he's probably right. Don't that beat all?"

"I can understand the jealousy," said Mama. "I was the kid sister myself, once."

Mama shot Aunt Theresa a knowing look. Aunt Theresa seemed surprised.

"Well, maybe you're right," she said slowly. "But they're so *young*. Barely thirteen."

"I was only twelve and you were seventeen when you began dating Joe Boudreau—remember?"

"I remember the time you put sand in his convertible top so we'd get a shower whether he put it up or left it down. But that was just a kid trick."

"Kid trick, nothing. *I* wanted Joe! I can laugh about it now, but I'm afraid my feelings were real enough then."

"You stinker!" Aunt Theresa hugged Mama. Then she kissed her cheek. "I guess that doesn't excuse Minnie's rather . . . rather extreme behavior, though, does it?" Aunt Theresa concluded.

Chapter Fourteen

New Names and Old

Hannah was not surprised that her parents had a long, serious talk in the kitchen that evening when Papa got home. Though she kept busy in the dining room, without intentionally snooping, Hannah caught bits and pieces enough of her parents' conversation to know they were talking about Minnie.

"But that wouldn't be fair to Miquie," Hannah heard Mama protest when Papa suggested they pack both mice onto the Greyhound for Boston the next morning, Thursday, two days early.

In the weeks that followed, Mama gradually gave Hannah bits and pieces of her talk with Papa. She told enough, anyway, so that Hannah pretty much figured out why things turned out the way they did during the two days after Minnie ran away.

"I think the Lord put those girls in our care, Harry, so He could use us to help them—perhaps with a problem even their parents don't understand," Mama had told Papa that evening.

"Their parents *could* understand them if only they'd pay attention to them, you know," Papa asserted. "Their father spends so much time away from home on business he hardly knows which twin is which."

"Well," said Mama, "*we* have our own children to rear. I'm sure the Lord put us on this island to give Hannah and Walter the personal attention they need. We can pray for the girls, though."

Papa rubbed his chin in thought. "The competition between those two girls has gone entirely too far," he said. "Walt doesn't like being the object of their rivalry, and I don't blame him. Perhaps we should do more than just pray."

"So we've got two problems," Mama murmured.

"You're right," Papa agreed. "Jealousy over which twin gets more attention and a craving for male attention."

"That looks like a long-term problem to me." Mama looked concerned.

"True. But maybe we can do something to steer things in the right direction. I've got an idea. First, I'm phoning Walt. I'm going to suggest that he stay with his aunt and uncle in Laketon until Saturday when we take his cousins to the mainland to catch the Boston bus. Second, I think it's time those girls had new names and separate identities. Millicent and Monique are what their parents named them, right?"

"You've never been much to remember kids' names," Mama laughed, "but those *are* their real names."

"Well, Millicent and Monique will be their names while they're with us. They haven't used them for so long they'll seem new, I'm sure," Papa affirmed.

❋ ❋ ❋ ❋ ❋ ❋ ❋

"Indian summer this is called, isn't it Papa?" Hannah smiled as she peered into the robin's egg blue sky that made a canopy over Moosehead's deep blue which stretched to the vast green forest spangled with the fall reds and yellows of maples. Hannah stood with Papa on the dock of Beaver Lodge the next morning as she helped him load bags for guests returning to the mainland.

"We won't see days like this again until spring," Papa agreed. "Weatherman says this'll continue only through the weekend, when a cold front will move in from Canada. This would be a good day for you and Monique to go camping with that two-man tent Aunt Theresa bought you for your birthday."

"Monique—Miquie? But what about Minnie?"

"There's room for only two in that tent. Millicent will have to wait until she visits us next time to camp out," Papa said evenly. "And by the way, please try to use your cousins' real names for the next couple of days—it's a little experiment Mama and I are working on, and we need your help."

"But what about Min . . . Millicent? You're not?!"

"No, Hannah." Papa tousled Hannah's wavy hair, which she hadn't yet braided that morning. *"Both* girls are staying until Saturday, as planned. Between me and Mama, though, I think we can keep Millicent busy," said Papa. "And one more thing."

"What's that?"

"Don't mention our plans to Monique until after I leave with the guests for Laketon. I'm taking Millicent along for the ride, and we'll probably do some shopping."

"Anything else I should not talk about with Monique, Papa?"

Hannah was aware that she had heard more of her parents' conversation in the kitchen Wednesday evening than she was supposed to hear. She feared that Monique might try to pry the details out of her.

"Don't mention *mice*," Papa chuckled. "We're trying to get those girls to see themselves as *individuals*, created special by God in *His* image rather than in each other's image."

"Ooo-o-oh, I *love* this, Uncle Harry," cooed Millicent, a.k.a. Minnie, later that morning in Laketon. She had gone to Laketon with Papa when he took all the Beaver Lodge guests—except for a couple who wished to stay and fish—to their cars at the Laketon municipal dock.

"That would look nice on you, and you may have it if it fits." Papa checked the fabric tag on the pink sweatshirt his niece had pulled off the rack at Northland Outfitters. The shirt had an outline map of Maine with a rainbow trout jumping on the end of a fishing line in the center. "Looks washfast," Papa said, satisfied that the shirt was of good material. "And would you like to go trout fishing?" he added, pointing at the trout.

"Would I *ever*," Millicent squealed. "But I don't have a Maine license."

"They sell them right here, Millicent," Papa answered. "I think I can afford a three-day license for you," he chuckled.

"Hey, here's one just like it, only powder blue," Millicent cried. "Miquie would love it. I can buy it and she'll pay me back." Millicent held the sweat-shirts up together.

Twins, Papa mouthed silently, viewing the near-identical shirts. "Tell you what, Millicent. I'm buy-ing the sweatshirts for both of you. You got to choose yours, so I get to pick out Monique's. Okay?"

"Okay."

Papa thought Millicent sounded just a mite dis-appointed. But he quickly picked a sweatshirt off the same rack in the same size as Millicent's pink one. It was forest green, and a moosehead was splashed across the top, with the slogan, "Moose-head Lake, Maine."

"Think she'll like this?"

"Sure," Millicent muttered.

"Why do you keep calling me Millicent, Uncle Harry?" the younger niece asked a few minutes later as, carrying the two shirts, a fishing license, and a new casting rod, she and Papa walked toward their boat at the village dock.

"Isn't that your name?" Papa sounded surprised.

"Yes, but..." Millicent could not think of a good answer.

"But?"

"Well, I dunno." She kicked a rock, hurt her toe, and hopped on one foot the length of two sidewalk sections.

"Tell you what I think," Papa said. "You girls have been mice almost since you learned to squeak—uh, speak. Let's try your real names for a couple of days and see if it helps you sort out who you are. This business of both of you always want-ing the same thing at the same time can only lead to trouble."

"It drives the boys crazy," Millicent admitted, giggling nervously. "Especially since we both usually want the same guy."

"You're pretty perceptive. Now try this idea for a moment. You girls are sisters—you're not the same person. You don't occupy the same space. You don't have the same soul. You are each created in God's image, special to Him as an *individual* with unique talents, desires, and personalities," said Papa. "God does not create clones."

"Oh, Uncle, that's a lot to take in my little mouse brain all at once."

"True. For now, just digest as much of what I said as you can," Papa agreed. "One more thing."

"Uncle Harry?"

"Being in God's image means, among other things, that we have human brains, capable of creativity that far exceeds that of a mouse—or any animal. Maybe you've adopted the wrong identity."

"Well, for this afternoon I guess my identity is 'fisherman,' or maybe 'fisherperson,'" Millicent sighed.

"Why not 'fishertwin'?" Papa teased.

"'Cause then I wouldn't really be me, would I, Uncle Harry?"

"Do we *hafta* be called by our real names, Unca Harry?" squeaked Monique at lunchtime that Thursday, putting on her poutiest, mousiest animal voice. Since Millicent and Hannah were waiting on tables while Mama cooked, Papa sat with his older niece to eat lunch and tell her what was going on. Monique did not think she should have to give up her nickname, since it was her younger sister, not she, who had run away.

"This won't work unless you *both* go along with it," Papa said firmly. "God deals with us as individuals," he added. "To ask one twin to stop being a mouse for two days while the other sister insists on being a mouse isn't going to work, is it?"

"Well, I suppose not," Monique admitted. "But I'm Miquie Mouse again the minute I leave here."

"Donald Duck, if you wish," Papa laughed.

"I think it's a great idea," put in Millicent, who came by to pour Papa more coffee. "I get to have Uncle Harry all to myself for the afternoon while he teaches me to fly fish for trout!"

"Oh?" Monique eyed Papa suspiciously. "Are you taking me fishing tomorrow?"

Papa's eyes were now laughing under his bushy eyebrows. "I doubt that there'll be time," he said. "I thought you wanted to go camping with Hannah ever since you arrived here last week. Your camping trip will keep you until mid-afternoon tomorrow."

"Hannah says her tent isn't big enough for the three of us," Monique commented.

"True. Not even if two of you are mice," Papa said.

"What's *that* supposed to mean?" Monique seemed puzzled.

"It means," Papa said slowly, "that Hannah has waited all summer for *one* girl who could camp out with her alone. Now's your chance to be that girl, since Millicent and I will fish until dark tonight. And tomorrow at dawn she will be learning how to milk a cow with me in the barn."

"But," Monique protested, "when do *I* get to be with you, Uncle Harry?"

"You've got a point." Papa looked worried, but only for a moment. "Tell you what. Have a good time camping until tomorrow afternoon. Be back here by three o'clock. I've got to take our last two guests to Laketon then. You can come along, and we'll have supper together in the dining room of the Northeastland Hotel. Their Friday specialty is all the fresh brook trout you can eat. Is it a date?"

"Cool!" Monique's dark eyes shined with glee.

Chapter Fifteen

Walt's Wheels

"Can you drive a car, Wal-*ter*?" Uncle Joe Boudreau was one of Walt's favorite people. Walt was enjoying the two days away from his cousins in Laketon with Uncle Joe and Aunt Theresa. The Boudreaus had no children, and they treated Walt and Hannah like royalty when they visited.

Walt did not like to be called Walter except by Mama and Papa. It bugged him especially to hear Uncle Joe, with his French Canadien accent, emphasize the second syllable of his name.

"Sorta," Walt answered. "I drive the John Deere tractor and the snowmobile. So I guess a car isn't much different. My name's Walt," he added quietly.

"Sorta, eh?" chuckled Uncle Joe. "And ze young man, he is growing up, *non*? I don't like it to be called Jo-*seph,* either. And you are handy with ze tools, *non*?"

Walt didn't know just what Uncle Joe was getting at, so he was silent for a moment.

"Yeah," he said at last, "I guess I'm pretty good

with tools. I can usually fix Papa's John Deere or
the snowmobile unless it's something major."

"Your island, it now has a road. So it needs an
auto, *non?*"

What *is* Uncle Joe leading up to? Walt was puzzled. Beaver Island had had a tractor and horse
road clear across it before Walt's family had moved
there. And Sam Sampson, with Papa's permission,
had in recent weeks used a chain saw to cut a
rough tractor road behind Bald Hill. Sam had connected it to Papa's logging road so that, using
Papa's tractor, he could haul home several loads of
firewood Papa had sold him. Papa jokingly called
this new road Sampson Street.

"How about a truck? You could be ze chau-*ffeur.
Your* truck, *non?*"

Uncle Joe had finally gained Walt's attention.

"Sounds like a winner," Walt said, still not sure
where this was leading.

"My old Chevy. She is yours, if you wish to fix
her up."

"Your truck? Don't you need it for the *President
Lincoln II*—for winter excursions on the ice?" Walt
was startled.

Uncle Joe laughed. *"Non*—no! Ze rivair boat, she
is only for water use from now on. Too much trouble to take her off ze boat and mount her on ze
truck. So ze old truck, she is all yours—if your Papa
will let you drive her on Bevair Island."

"Hey, Papa'll let me, soon's the lake freezes solid.
That truck's a four-wheel drive, isn't it?"

"Sure is," agreed Uncle Joe.

"We can sure use something besides the John
Deere during cold weather. Winter is when Papa
has to haul big stuff across the ice—stuff too big to

bring in the boat. But I can't get a driver's license because I'm not sixteen yet," Walt worried.

"Don't need one," Uncle Joe assured Walt. "A license is for *public* roads, *non?* You'll be driving only on ice and *private* roads. And Hannah, she can learn to drive, too."

Walt followed Uncle Joe to a shed behind his garage where the old pickup truck, its nose in the shed to protect it from the weather, was parked with its bare frame poking into the backyard.

"Ze body and ze cab, zey are in ze junkyard," Uncle Joe apologized. "I took zem off to bolt the *President Lincoln II* onto her," he explained. "But she has got a seat and steering wheel, like a trac-*tor*. She will do your work on ze island, *non?*"

"*Non*—I mean *oui*—yes," stammered Walt.

Walt had expected to find a complete truck, though he knew his uncle had had it apart once before. Here was just a bare frame, four wheels, and an engine. The truck body, fenders, and cab were badly rusted when he'd last seen them, true enough. So there were no holes to patch. In fact, there was *nothing* left to patch!

"Wow!" was all Walt could think of to say.

"You like her?" Uncle Joe asked.

"Well . . . well, I guess so. Yeah, sure. It'll make a great truck for the island."

Walt was surprised and a little disappointed, but he wasn't about to let his prize get away.

"Want to see her run?" Uncle Joe asked.

"Sure." *Will it run?* Walt had wanted to ask. He was relieved that he hadn't had to.

"Battery's on my bench in ze garage, hooked up to my charger," Uncle Joe explained. "If you will get it, I will clean ze corrosion off ze cables."

Uncle Joe pulled out his pocketknife and bent over a wooden box bolted beside the truck engine, where two ratty-looking battery cables hung.

Walt had no trouble with the battery and charger. Papa had gotten a charger like Uncle Joe's right after he installed a generator on Beaver Island. By the time Walt returned, Uncle Joe was ready with the cables.

"Want to fire her up?" Uncle Joe asked.

"Yeah!" Walt hopped aboard onto a plank that had an old kitchen chair bolted to it under the steering wheel. He pumped the gas pedal as he had seen Papa and Mama do when they started the Buick they owned with Aunt Theresa. Walt grabbed the key and turned it.

The truck engine ground over a few times, then started with a deafening roar.

"Let up on ze gas!!"

Walt lifted his foot off. The motor continued to run, still noisy, but quieter.

"What's the matter?" Walt shouted over the din. "Did I ruin it?"

"*Non, non.* No harm. Just needs a muffler. Back her into ze yard."

Walt found reverse, and the truck lurched backward.

"Now drive her around front!" Uncle Joe hopped onto the plank and grabbed a pipe that he had bolted across where the dashboard used to be.

Walt started with a lurch, stalled the engine, then restarted it. On the second try he got the hang of it, and soon he was driving as smoothly as if this were the familiar John Deere. Walt followed the wheel tracks around to the front and parked in the driveway.

❋ ❋ ❋ ❋ ❋ ❋ ❋

"Cool!"

Walt ignored the soft female voice for a moment. Lying on your back with loose rust from an old exhaust pipe dropping into your eyes isn't exactly a fun place to talk with a girl. Walt had changed the truck's oil and spark plugs. Then he'd spent several hours with Uncle Joe's hacksaw and electric drill building a frame of pipes to support two new exhaust pipes and new mufflers. This was the fourth time he'd loosened the muffler clamp, trying to line the pesky pipe up.

"Cool," the voice cooed again. "You've built a real exhaust stack, like on a big semi-truck. Gonna add an air horn?"

Crossly, Walt rolled partway over to see who was flapping her lip while he tried to work. The pixie perched on Uncle Joe's split-rail yard fence only grinned at him, showing a perfect set of white teeth. Her long, thick hair, like her lips, was red, not blood red, but the marvelous rust shade of autumn leaves. Her alabaster skin, lightly dusted with freckles, was not used to the sun. City girl, Walt decided, and this made him nervous. He'd seen her once before, though, with her parents last Sunday in church. She seemed to be about his age.

"An air horn," she repeated when he only squinted at her from beneath the old truck. She grinned again, tugging at an imaginary cord above her head.

Walt and Hannah had played that game for hundreds of miles on the way to New York last year. Every time Papa would pass a semi they'd pretend to yank a cord. Usually the driver would yank back with a terrific, loud blast of air to liven up the journey.

"Hon-n-nk! hon-n-nk!" Walt said, starting to sit up. He cracked his head on the skeleton truck's steel frame. "Ouch!" Walt lay back down, then made groaning noises, pretending he was about to die.

"You goin' to make it?" The pixie on the fence didn't giggle, like his cousins. She didn't sound alarmed, either.

"Yeah," said Walt, grabbing his wrench again. "Gimmie a hand, will y'?"

"Sure." The girl jumped down and bounded onto the truck. Walt could see that she was petite, not long and lean like his sister. She grabbed the new muffler, which hung loosely in a new clamp. "Where d' y' want it?" she asked, showing no offense at Walt's abrupt demand for help.

"Lift it a bit."

"Okay." She lifted.

"Awright, now hold it there while I tighten these nuts."

"It's a cherry bomb muffler, isn't it?" the girl asked as she gripped the small, bright red muffler. "My sister's boyfriend's got a cherry bomb on his car. Makes so much racket the cops are always pullin' him over. They sound mellow, though."

"I won't get bothered by the police for this one," Walt remarked from underneath as he put his muscle onto the wrench handle. "This truck's goin' to Beaver Island on the ice soon's the lake freezes."

"Ice? You can drive on the ice? Where we used to live, in Connecticut, you can't drive on the ice."

"Well, it's different here in Maine." Walt grabbed the frame with both hands and pulled himself out. "Name's Walt Parmenter," he said, wiping the grease off his forehead with his sleeve.

"I'm Caylin Coulson," the smiling girl with the garnet hair said. "We moved up here in September. How come I don't see you at Laketon Christian Academy—you were in church?" Caylin asked, sounding sincerely interested.

I like that, thought Walt, still cautious but no longer suspicious. *No flirting. Just friendly. Nice, too.*

"I live on Beaver Island," he said, pointing to the pine-studded isle across the blue lake. "My sis and I, we go to school at home."

Chapter Sixteen

Bearly Camping

"That's barely camping," chuckled Mama, when Hannah told her that she and Monique, a.k.a. Miquie, would tent that night on the wooden floor of the old logger's cabin. "When your Papa and I were married, we camped out in Baxter State Park under the stars."

"You didn't use our old tent?" Hannah was surprised, for she knew Papa had years earlier cut up what he called the honeymoon tent to make a tarp to cover some machinery.

"We had left the tent stakes in Skowhegan," Mama admitted. "So it was the second night before we could make new ones to set the tent up. But we didn't have an air mattress," she said, eyeing the box Hannah had just toted from the supply room.

"All the comforts of home, Mama," Hannah teased. "And we're taking Papa's gas stove and the lantern, too. He says not to build a bonfire 'cause it's been too dry."

Though Papa had said that Hannah could take the tractor, since it was more than a mile to the

112

back of the island where the girls planned to camp, both girls decided they'd rather ride Ebony. Mama thought they should hitch Ebony to the buggy, but Hannah protested that riding in a saddle is more fun, and they could still pack enough stuff for one night by tying it into sacks slung over the horse's back.

"Hannah's right," Papa agreed. "Ebony's a big horse, and it's not that far."

"'Sides, we'll take turns, Mama," said Hannah. "I'll let Monique ride ahead of me in the saddle, once she gets the hang of it."

"You'll need these." Papa passed Hannah a length of clothesline rope and a burlap feed sack. "Any food you don't eat tonight for supper," he added, "hoist it about ten feet up—use that big old maple by the ruins of the cabin. Bears can't bother your food that way."

"Are there *bears?!*" Monique looked scared.

"Coons, skunks—whatever will eat your breakfast. Guess I shoulda mentioned that Sam Sampson shot that old she-bear. He caught it in his pigpen."

"I *knew* that, Papa!" Hannah answered hotly.

Papa looked at her reprovingly, and with her eyes Hannah apologized. She hadn't meant to speak so impatiently to her father, but she knew bears are something you don't dare even *mention* if you're taking a city cousin deep into the Maine woods. Papa hadn't intended to let "bear" slip out, but it was too late for him to take it back.

"The old bear *is* dead," Hannah emphasized. "Anyway, plain ol' eastern black bears won't attack humans," she calmly added.

Through Hannah's memory, though, raced the picture of the two cute, round-eared cubs she had seen with their mother in the blueberry patch on Bald Hill. What had become of them?

"Make him gallop, Hannah," Monique cried. Ebony had now brought Hannah and her cousin to the long stretch of flat, soft soil made of clay and rotting corduroy logs next to Juniper Bog. Hannah knew there were no rocks here for a horse to stumble over, so she loosened the reins and dug her heels in.

"Whee-e-e-e!" squealed Monique, "I like this!"

"Arf," agreed Hunter, racing alongside Ebony's flank.

"Sure is fun," Hannah panted. She reined Ebony in now, for they had reached rough terrain. The sun hung low in the west, and the pines and firs cast long shadows across the old logging road.

A dark, furry animal waddled across the road, and Hannah stood up in the stirrups for a better look. The creature was gone before horse and girls arrived there, and Ebony, unconcerned, trotted right past.

"C'mon, Hunter," Hannah called, whistling, as the silly hound plunged into the underbrush after the beast. Hunter obediently returned, panting. Hannah suddenly realized that ten fingers were digging into her ribs in terror. "What was *that?*" Monique whispered hoarsely.

"Coon, I think. Now will you *please* loosen up. You're goin' t' have my sides so black and blue I'll look like Ebony bucked me off."

Monique relaxed her grip. "Will coons hurt people?"

"No. But like Papa says, they'll make a mess of your food supply."

The girls were soon at the ruins of the old cabin in a clearing near the lake. Here they found that Walt, months earlier, had torn the small building down to the bare floor. He had used a few of the wallboards to patch the floor, then burned the rest of the ruins.

"Neat!" cried Monique, when she saw the floor, level on a rock foundation. "Just like a tent platform at a state park."

"Neat, maybe," Hannah cautiously agreed. "Last time I was here, there was a porcupine under this old cabin floor, and we brought Hunter home with his nose full of porcupine quills." She tied Ebony to a tree, leaving their camping equipment still loaded on his back.

"C'mon, Hunt," Hannah now commanded, "let's do your stuff."

Snapping his leash onto his collar, Hannah led Hunter around the stone foundation. He sniffed at a few holes but made no move to dig under the floor.

"No porcupines or skunks under there, eh? Chipmunks or field mice, maybe?"

"Mice?" Monique said. "Br-r-r-r!"

"I thought you liked mice?"

"I do. In the 'toons. But without Minnie here to help me squeak, it takes the fun out of it. Wonder what kind of noise a moose makes?"

Monique stretched the front of her sweatshirt with her hands, glancing at the broad-antlered creature on the front.

"A moose goes 'splash, splash,'" laughed Hannah. "I know. I nearly crashed into one once. The big, ugly critter was eating water weeds in the lake on a foggy morning."

"Yeah? Tell me about it."

"Tell you later. Let's unload Ebony and get the tent up. It's getting dark."

The moon was a mere sliver of silver over Moosehead Lake, and a soft south breeze kept the night unusually warm for October in the north woods. Hannah and Monique soon found two large blocks of maple logs that Papa's logging crew had once used as chairs around their campfire. The girls rolled them onto the old floor in front of their open tent. A third block they used as a table, on which they set Papa's gas camp stove.

"This is super," exclaimed Monique as she relaxed while toasting a marshmallow over the gas stove.

"And no mosquitoes," chuckled Hannah. "Did y' notice?"

"I guess the mosquitoes go home on Labor Day, like the tourists," Monique joked.

"Actually, it's the frost that gets 'em. If we get a good freeze, it kills the mosquitoes. Then if there's Indian summer weather, like now, you're not bothered by the biting little beasties."

"I guess that means we can go swimming without being bothered," said Monique. "C'mon."

"But the water's like ice this time o' year. 'Sides, we didn't bring swimsuits," Hannah protested.

"I brought extra jeans to wear back tomorrow. Didn't you?"

"Well, yes."

"Let's go." Monique slipped off her sneakers and wriggled out of her sweatshirt, under which she wore a tee shirt.

The loggers had left a long pine log, chipped flat on top with an axe, as a bridge out to a big rock in the lake. It didn't take much for Hannah and Monique to figure out that it had been rigged for swimming. Monique raced ahead, and she was at the water before Hannah—who had not expected her city cousin to dive into near-freezing water—could get ready.

"Wait!" Hannah screamed, seeing Monique racing out onto the log. "Don't dive until you know it's deep enough!"

Monique dived anyway.

Hannah ran out to the rock. No sign of her cousin.

Then, way out, a dark head appeared. Monique bobbed to the surface and turned over, swimming away from shore with a backstroke.

"How's the water?" Hannah hollered.

"All right, once you get in. But you're gonna freeze if you try to wade in slowly. 'Fraid t' get y' little pinkies wet?"

I'm going to wish I'd brought my wet suit, Hannah silently considered. Out loud she asked, "Is it deep enough to dive from this rock?"

"I dove right in, and I didn't touch bottom," said Monique.

"Awright." Hannah dived in. The chill numbed her, but she found that Monique was right. The water temperature was tolerable once your body adjusted.

The girls found the rock too slippery with moss to climb onto from the lake. So they swam to shore and shivering, waded up the rocky beach.

Suddenly Hannah and Monique froze in their tracks. A thief stood beneath the bag of food that Hannah had pulled up into a tree. The uninvited guest seemed to be trying to reach their bag in the near darkness, but his arms were just a bit too short.

In silent terror Hannah now wished she'd brought Walt's shotgun.

"Hey, why don't y' just climb the tree?" shrieked Monique, angry at the prowler, who seemed as stupid as he was bold.

Hannah clamped her hand across Monique's mouth.

"He may have a gun or a knife," Hannah warned her cousin, who, though older, was somewhat smaller than she.

Hunter, who had followed a rabbit trail into the woods just before the girls dived into the lake, suddenly shot into the clearing. "R-R-R-R-R-ARF! ARF! ARF!" Hannah's hound lunged straight at the robber, a burly fellow in a black suit.

Then a *second* thief appeared, hurrying from the tent, snapping in his hungry jaws a half-eaten hamburger left from the girls' supper.

"Robber!" screamed Monique, her sense leaving her again. "I was going to eat that before bed," she yelled.

The twin thieves, both dressed in black fur, now tore toward the woods, crashing noisily through dry brush left from the old logging operation, going now on all four legs as they loped along. As the bear cubs passed Ebony, the terrified horse reared and snapped his tether rope. Then the girls' ride home thundered down the logging road toward Beaver Lodge, his hoofbeats pounding wildly until they finally faded into the night.

"Your heart's thumping something hyper," Monique said at last.

"So's yours," Hannah said. Until now, neither girl realized how tightly they were hugging each other.

"How're we getting home?" moaned Monique.

"Walk, I guess. Papa will come after our gear with the tractor."

"I...I *can't* walk home in the dark. I'm scared o' bears!" Monique wailed. "What are we going to do?"

"Just what we'd planned to do. Hunter'll bite the fierce ol' bears if they come back."

Hannah stooped to pat Hunter, who, tongue out and panting, had just returned from chasing the hungry cubs, who were more scared than the girls.

"We'll sleep in the tent with Hunter between us. Then we'll have breakfast in the morning."

"But he has fleas!"

"So do bears."

"I'm afraid of bears," Monique shuddered.

"You said that once before. They're *only* cubs," Hannah stated, calmer now. "Truthfully, though they make me nervous."

The sun had been up more than an hour when girls and hound finally poked their nervous noses outside the tent. The sky was cloudless, and the wind, blowing south in the evening, had turned due north, bringing a frost that whitened the grass. The wet clothes from swimming, which Hannah and Monique had left draped across the wooden-block chairs, were frozen so stiff that they had to be carefully pried loose to keep them from tearing.

"S'pose Ebony's safe in the barn?" Monique queried, sadly eyeing the horse's broken tether rope.

"Safe," Hannah assured her. "But not in the barn. We'll find him by the back pasture gate, I reckon."

"We're goin' back to the lodge this morning, aren't we?" Monique sounded worried.

"You want t'?" Hannah was not sure whether Monique was worried they'd stay or worried they'd go home too soon.

"After last night? *Bears!*" Monique trembled. "I want to go home soon's we eat breakfast."

"Okay. You start the stove. I'll get the bacon down from the tree," Hannah said. With Hunter trotting at her heels, Hannah hurried to where she had hauled the bag of food up out of reach of bears and untied the rope.

※ ※ ※ ※ ※ ※ ※

Half an hour's hike brought Hannah and Monique to where the road pitched downhill toward Juniper Bog.

"There's where I found that herd of potbellied pigs," Hannah explained, pointing to a clump of alders and beeches on the edge of the wetland. "We came past here on Ebony so fast yesterday that I didn't get to show you."

"That's no pig—*OH!*" Monique squeaked suddenly.

"Shush," said Hannah. "Don't move. Nothing to be afraid of. I expect he may recognize your shirt."

Hannah suppressed her own fright and grinned as she glanced at the bull moose on the front of Monique's new green sweatshirt. The creature that appeared before the campers was a bull moose, all right, and he had just come down Bald Hill.

"ARF!" Hunter offered his opinion of the big, gangly, long-legged fellow with the antlers.

The moose leaped and crossed the old logging road in one bound. It seemed to Hannah as if half of Bald Hill had suddenly shot into the air. That moose was *huge.* It disappeared into the brush with a crashing that seemed to go on forever.

✳ ✳ ✳ ✳ ✳ ✳ ✳

"That bear after our food was eight feet tall *at least,*" Monique bragged to Millicent later that morning. She talked so much about her trip with Hannah that, as Mama said later, "You could hardly get a word in edgewise if it were shaved off with a razor blade."

"Bear cubs *do* grow up rather fast," Papa agreed. "I think I'd better get the game warden to hunt those critters with a stun gun and take them to the mainland before they get any bigger," he added.

"Hannah, I want to go camping with you again *next* year," Monique squealed. "We had the most *fun!*"

"*You an' I* will go fishin' next year again, won't we, Uncle Harry," said Millicent. "They can have their mean ol' bears and big bull moose!"

"If there's going to be any camping or fishing ever again for anybody, Hannah," Mama admonished, "you'd better help Papa go get your tent and gear with the tractor and trailer right away."

"I'll take the three of you," Papa chuckled. "I've got a big dinner date in Laketon this afternoon," he said, winking at Monique. "So let's get started."

Chapter Seventeen

Good Fences Make Good Neighbors

"We sure can use another vehicle on the island," Papa said, resting his foot on the truck bumper as he watched Walt work. It was Saturday morning, and the Parmenters had come to Laketon to say good-bye to Monique and Millicent Mitchell as they boarded the bus for Boston. Papa had found Walt working on his truck, parked next to Uncle Joe's garage.

"She's a four-wheel drive, Papa." Walt was beaming as he wiped the grease from his hands. "Uncle Joe has given me a set of tire chains—says she'll go through knee-deep snow." Walt grinned, then turned toward the red-haired girl perched on the old chair that served as a truck seat. "Try 'er now," he said.

The girl turned the key and the motor came to life. She gunned the engine three or four times, grinning impishly at the throaty rumble of the dual cherry bomb mufflers Walt had installed, as if the work were her own creation.

"Perfect," Walt said. "Kill it."

The girl shut the motor off.

"Uncle Joe showed me how to adjust the timing to make it run smooth," Walt said, plainly pleased with his success.

"Who's your helper?" Papa nodded toward the girl.

"Oh, uh, this here's Caylin, Papa. Caylin Coulson. Her family just started goin' to our church. Sorry. I shoulda introduced her sooner."

"I think I met your father, Caylin," said Papa. "Mark Coulson, isn't it?"

"Yes, it is. And my mother is Grace." Caylin answered with such poise and graciousness that Papa couldn't help thinking that she ought to have been named Grace also.

And, too, Papa understood Walt's embarrassment at introducing Caylin. A girl like that could make a fellow feel self-conscious and awkward. Yet she could also make a guy feel like a man. What a contradiction! Papa thought.

"We've brought Monique and Millicent over to catch the Greyhound," said Papa. "I think you should come inside and say good-bye."

"The mice?" Walt was not used to hearing his cousins' real names.

"They are *girls*," Papa corrected. "I expect they've learned something about their identities in the last two days," he added, chuckling.

"I'd love to meet your cousins," said Caylin. Walter had told her only a few details about why he was staying with his aunt and uncle while his cousins were visiting at Beaver Island.

"C'mon," Walt sighed.

"We've made real Maine-iacs out of ze twins,"

chuckled Uncle Joe to Papa, as Papa, Caylin, and Walt entered the house. Monique and Millicent were enjoying a video tape of a Moosehead Lake fishing derby on the living room TV.

"I offered to let them watch the Saturday-morning cartoons if they preferred," Uncle Joe explained.

Caylin, who had been in Hannah's Sunday school class, just then spotted Hannah in the kitchen with Mama and Aunt Theresa. She slipped into the kitchen to say hello.

"Hi, Walt," said Monique, who had turned around at the sound of their uncle's voice. "We gotta leave today. Sorry we can't stay longer."

"I'm sorry we're leaving, too," Millicent put in. She paused awkwardly, studying Walt with her clear brown eyes. "And what I did was really, really dumb," she added. "I don't blame you for being mad."

"I forgive you," said Walt. Growing up with a sister had taught Walt a few things about being nice to people, and he realized it was time to make up. "Have a good trip to Boston," he added, holding out his hand to shake hers.

Millicent grabbed Walt's hand, but before he could stop her she kissed him firmly on the cheek. She then raced toward the hallway, where she'd left her suitcase.

Caylin stepped out of the kitchen just then, crashing right into Millicent. Caylin went sprawling.

"Sorry!" Millicent squeaked, becoming a mouse for only a moment. She grabbed Caylin's arm and helped her up.

"That's okay," Caylin laughed. "I came inside just to meet you. I'm Caylin."

"Caylin goes to my Sunday school class," explained Hannah. "Her family moved in here next to Uncle Joe and Aunt Theresa in September."

"Oh, I remember. We were in the same class last Sunday morning," said Millicent, regaining her composure.

"And I'm Monique. Remember me?"

Caylin looked puzzled. "Hey," she cried, "the mice—Minnie and Miquie, like at Disneyland."

"Yeah," agreed Millicent. "'Cept we've decided to be *people* from now on."

"Created in God's own image, a little lower than the angels, like Uncle Harry says," Monique piped. "*Not* animals."

* * * * * * *

"I think," said Papa, watching Walt, Caylin, and Hannah say good-bye to Millicent and Monique as the Greyhound was loading, "that Walt's staying away from those girls for a couple of days did both him and the twins some good."

"Wasn't it the poet Robert Frost who said, 'Good fences make good neighbors?'" Mama asked. "When we set proper limits for behavior, we get along much better," she added. "That's what Frost meant, I think, and it seemed to work with the kids."

"Which reminds me," Papa said, "I promised Sam Sampson I'd get us a couple of rolls of fence wire at the Agway Farm & Feed Store today."

"Us?" Mama queried.

"Yeah. I'm helping Sam build a pig-proof fence along our property line. I've agreed to buy a roll of wire if he buys one."

"Did he give you the money?" Mama asked suspiciously.

"No," admitted Papa. "Sam is becoming Beaver Lodge's part-time handyman. With Walt gone, I learned how short-handed I really am, now that the extra business is keeping me tied up with our guests. I agreed to take the cost of one roll of wire out of Sam's pay. I'll pay for the other, since this is a joint project."

The Sampson children, Mell and little Paul, had become regular boat passengers of Hannah's family for a ride to Sunday school since the week they arrived on Beaver Island. They usually took their baths for church at Beaver Lodge with Hannah's help. Though the old Sampson place had a bathroom, the windmill with its water tank had rusted and collapsed many years ago. Papa had permitted Sam to hitch a garden hose to his pump house which Sam ran around Bald Hill into his own backyard. So with no indoor water supply, and only what hot water Judith Sampson's teakettle could heat, the Sampson children did not get regular baths.

Hannah had solved the problem of having Melanie and Paul clean for Sunday school by inviting the children each Saturday afternoon to help her tend her own ten pigs and feed Papa's calves. She would then treat them to a hot bath in one of Beaver Lodge's several bathrooms. Once in a while, they would spend the night, Paul rolled up in a blanket on the rug on Hannah's bedroom floor and Mell sharing Hannah's large, comfortable bed. On such occasions, Hunter, who ordinarily slumbered his doggy dreams away on top of Hannah's quilt, was banished to the floor, where he curled up next to little Paul on the braided rug.

Mama also had built bridges into the Sampson home and hearts. Sometimes she would bake the family a pie. Once she taught Judith how to use a paint roller to paint ceilings that hadn't seen fresh paint in thirty years. Mama gave Mrs. Sampson several dozen canning jars, since Beaver Lodge now had a freezer; and with Hannah's assistance, Mama helped Judith can fruits and vegetables during the weeks of autumn. Many of these foods were left over from the Parmenters' own garden.

With Papa now in daily contact with his part-time employee, Sam, the association with the Sampsons was complete. Walt, too, often worked alongside Sam, building fences, repairing the Beaver Lodge dock, or even building a shelter for Sam's Vietnamese pigs out of boards salvaged from the ruins of the old Sampson barn.

Hannah peered out across the porch one late October day to see Sam coming with Papa's John Deere. Odd, she thought, Walt's supposed to be using the tractor to haul supplies to where Papa and Sam are building a fence.

Then Hannah noticed that Walt was crouched in the trailer behind the tractor. He seemed intent on aiding someone—it was Papa!

"Mama!" Hannah screamed. "Papa's hurt!"

Sam was at the front steps by the time Mama rushed out. He pulled the John Deere up, leaving the engine idling while Mama clambered aboard the trailer.

"Stepped into a hole. Broke his leg," Sam explained tersely. Wisely, Sam waited in a porch chair, smoking a cigarette and fidgeting nervously while Mama took charge.

"Want me to call the Maine Forest Service's rescue helicopter, Mama?" Walt asked quickly.

"Don't," said Papa between gasps of pain. "Costs a fortune. Wait until we have an emergency."

"This *is* an emergency," Mama insisted.

"It's not...O-O-O-OHH!...not life threatening. Get me an ambulance," Papa groaned.

"Ambulances don't drive on water. Lake's not frozen yet," Walt pointed out. Is Papa delirious? Walt wondered.

"I...OUCH...know that." Papa gritted his teeth. "Get *them* to come to Laketon!"

"Hannah," Mama said, in control of her senses by now, "hop up here with your Papa. I'll phone the Foxcroft Community Hospital and have them meet us at the Laketon Village Dock with an ambulance."

"Walt, Sam," continued Mama. "You guys will need to lift Harry—*carefully*—into the big boat."

* * * * * * *

Papa came home next day in a wheelchair, his leg in a cast. Hannah was not surprised to see Sam trudge out of the path to the old Sampson place the moment Walt arrived at the dock with Mama and Papa. Sam hurried to the waterfront and lifted the wheelchair ashore while Walt and Mama helped Papa slide himself onto the dock.

"I guess things look pretty grim," said Papa. He had just led his family in prayer, while Sam quietly waited in the kitchen.

No one, however, seemed to know what to do next.

"Hunting season begins next week," said Papa. "Most of our hunting guests are from out of state."

"Which means," Walt added knowingly, "that they require a licensed guide, and their guide is sitting here with his leg broken."

"I shall phone them all and cancel their reservations this evening," Mama insisted. "Tomorrow I'll send their deposit money back."

Which means, Hannah said to herself, not daring to say it out loud, most of our fall income is gone. We will have a very lean winter indeed. And the Sampsons will starve, since Sam can't feed them on the little he earns from those pigs. Papa can't pay him if we don't have paying guests, that's for sure.

Chapter Eighteen

God's Surprising Answer

By the time Mama and Papa had finished discussing their family's predicament, Sam had quietly slipped out the kitchen door and shuffled off for home. Only one thing was decided that afternoon. At Papa's insistence, Mama agreed not to phone the hunting guests until the following evening.

"To wait 24 hours won't do any harm, and it will give us time to pray and trust the Lord for some direction. After tomorrow, though," Papa concluded, "it's only honest that we contact each of our guests so they can make other vacation plans."

"Mama," said Walt later that evening after he had milked Molly and fed the calves. "I heard an interesting news report on station WABI on the radio in the barn."

"What's that?"

Mama sounds discouraged, Hannah thought. It better be good, Walt, if you're going to cheer Mama up, she said to herself.

"Tomorrow's the last day to take the test for a Maine hunting guide's license—at ten o'clock in the Fish and Game Department in Augusta. I've read Papa's guide manual. I think I could pass the test, and maybe *some* of the guests will hire me to guide for them."

"Did you read the part about having to be eighteen to qualify for a guide's license?" asked Papa, who had been listening from the living room.

"It's a pipe dream," said Mama. "A guide needs *years* of woods experience, besides passing a written test."

"Son, come in the living room, please," Papa called from his wheelchair.

"Walt, I'm *sure* you can pass the written test," Papa said as soon as Walt was seated beside him. "And in a year or so you may be competent enough to be a guide. But the law says you must be eighteen." Papa tousled Walt's hair as Walt sat on the couch, his head hanging low.

Hannah was surprised next morning before dawn to find Sam in the kitchen with Mama when she came downstairs.

"My old lady, she wouldn't give me a minute's rest 'less I agreed to come tell you this," Sam said. He pulled out his wallet and laid it open on the kitchen table for Mama's inspection.

Mama put down a homemade doughnut she had, without enjoying it, been munching on. She leaned over for a closer look. "Why, it's a guide's license!" Mama showed just a bit of surprise, elation even, Hannah thought.

"But it's a New Hampshire license, and it's expired," Mama continued, her happiness sinking through the floor once again.

"Shore," said Sam, "shore 'tis. Did you hear the radio news last night?"

"About the last chance to take the guide's test being today? Walt heard it."

"You once held a New Hampshire guide's license?" Papa asked in surprise, wheeling his chair from the downstairs bathroom, where he'd been shaving.

"Yes, sir!"

"There's not much difference between their test and Maine's," Papa said thoughtfully.

"I expect so. My Judith's been onto me about it all night," Sam said yawning. "She says I'm not a man if I don't give it a shot."

"We-ell. Costs a hundred bucks," Papa said.

Sam looked crestfallen. "You know I ain't got that kind o' money."

"I think I can arrange an advance on your pay," Papa assured him. "And if you pass the test, you'll get to keep all the money from the hunting trips with my guests."

"And Beaver Lodge will be full of paying guests for a month—that's cash in *your* pocket, too," Sam smiled.

"I'm phoning Joe Boudreau right now to ask him to gas up the Buick and meet you at the dock at Laketon," Papa said. He grabbed the cellular phone from the kitchen table.

"I kin drive. No need to put yer brother-in-law out fer me," Sam fussed.

"It's two hours to Augusta," Papa pointed out. "You'll need every minute of it to study the Maine guide manual while Joe drives. Hannah," he added, "please go dig that manual out of my desk drawer for Sam here."

"Hannah, taste one of those doughnuts," chuck-led Mama, as soon as Sam hurried off into the still dark fall morning to take Papa's boat to Laketon.

Hannah bit one of the home-fried cakes from the bowl on the table. "Yec-c-chh! Where'd these come from?" She spat it out.

"Sam brought them," Mama said lightly. "His wife made them yesterday, so they *are* fresh."

"But they taste *awful*!"

"Agreed," laughed Mama. "Remember that old bear that Sam shot?"

"Mama, she didn't!"

"Cooked 'em in bear grease," Mama affirmed. "When Sam comes back from Augusta this after-noon, I'm going to reward him with half a gallon of cooking oil for Judith."

❊ ❊ ❊ ❊ ❊ ❊ ❊

Whether Sam, Papa, or Mama was the happiest when Sam came home with a Maine guide's license, no one could say for sure. But Papa's stake in the Maine fall tourist trade was saved. And the Sampson family would have money for winter clothes and a new waterline, both into the house and into Sam's pig barn.

Chapter Nineteen

An Island Thanksgiving

Hannah hunkered into her hooded parka as she watched the last of the deer hunters climb aboard the Hopper Chopper Service helicopter. A light dusting of snow blew around the front yard of Beaver Lodge, driven by the spinning blades of the big whirlybird as the aircraft lifted off for Laketon.

"Aren't they expensive, Papa?"

"You bet!" Papa smiled grimly, leaning on his crutches. "But the hunters seem willing enough to pay it." He motioned toward a large, fiberglass motorboat that Sam was about to haul ashore with the tractor to store until its owners came for it in the spring. "The lake ice would cut a boat like that in half before it got halfway across," said Papa. "And we've got another week or so of hunting season after Thanksgiving. If it weren't for the Hopper Chopper Company, we'd have had to shut down two weeks ago."

Hannah did not answer Papa as she selected a flat stone from an outcropping of shale on the edge of the front lawn. She threw the stone sidearm, hard as she could sling it. The rock struck the frozen lake in a skid, skittering through the light snow until it was nearly out of sight. Hannah picked up another, tossed it and caught it. Changing her mind, she dropped it. If I litter the ice with rocks, Hannah told herself, it'll ruin the skating. She considered how precious few days of clear ice were available for skating each fall before the winter snows blanketed the lake and it became necessary to shovel or plow before one could skate.

"Thanksgiving will have to be here on the island this year," Mama said as soon as Hannah entered the house.

"Yeah." Hannah sounded disappointed.

Since Hannah had been a very little girl, even when her family had lived in Skowhegan, Thanksgiving dinner had been an event at Uncle Joe and Aunt Theresa's in Laketon. Grandma had been alive when Hannah was small, and she had lived with Aunt Theresa.

But this year, an unseasonally early freeze had isolated Hannah's family on Beaver Island several weeks earlier than usual. The thin ice would destroy Papa's boats if he tried to use them, but it would not yet support a snowmobile. And Hopper Chopper's helicopter service was closed on Thanksgiving Day.

"Let's invite Sam Sampson and his family for Thanksgiving dinner."

Hannah held her breath, waiting for Papa to answer Mama's suggestion.

"They probably have their own dinner all planned," Papa said mildly.

Is he trying to talk Mama out of it—or just being logical? Hannah wondered.

"That is one reason I want to invite them," Mama explained. "I went over there this morning with that jacket of Mell's that I put a new zipper in. They don't have any meat in the house except a few lake trout Sam caught. And I don't think Judith knows how to bake a pie. Their Thanksgiving dinner plans will be rather thin, I'm afraid."

"Well," Papa agreed, rubbing his chin, "it would be a chance to show them some love. That's a commodity that seems lacking in that family."

"S'pose Sam shows up drunk?" It was Walt's turn to protest. Walt had once had to ask Sam to go home and sober up when he nearly fell off Papa's tractor while helping him do farmwork.

"That's a possibility," Mama admitted. "I wonder how Jesus would have ministered to a family if one of its members got drunk once in a while?"

"I don't think Jesus would have avoided them," Hannah said. She knew that Mama and Papa wanted her and Walt's opinion in such situations.

"Well," Papa said, "I vote to invite them. Can you plan dinner for twelve o'clock? Sam seldom drinks much until afternoon."

"Good idea," Walt agreed. "I'll go over right now, if Hannah will come with me."

"I'm bringing the kids back to take baths and spend the night, okay Mama?" said Hannah. "I can teach Mell to bake pies—her mother sure isn't going to."

"Little Paul's a brat," Walt protested. "Last time he spent an evening here he set to bawling in the barn and scared Molly so she wouldn't give her milk."

"Why don't I read Paul a Thanksgiving story while you milk the cow?" Papa suggested. "I've even got one knee he can sit on while I read." Papa patted his unbroken left leg as he sat down in a reclining rocker.

Thanksgiving dinner was a surprise for both the Parmenters and the Sampsons. Judith Sampson had taken her children to pick a peck of cranberries from a wild patch on Juniper Bog. Her husband had discovered them years earlier when he had illegally trapped beaver there. If Judith could not bake pies, her cranberry sauce was equal to the best.

Though Mama had believed the Sampsons were to be without meat, except fish, Sam had a large buck hanging on the back porch, given to him by one of his guiding customers who wanted only the head for a trophy. Judith and Sam had taken turns stocking their woodstove all night to create a perfectly delicious rib roast.

Mell managed to get her arms covered in pumpkin pie batter clear to her elbows during Hannah's pie-baking lessons. The ambitious girls baked not only for dinner but also enough to keep the family supplied for a week afterward. Fresh whipped Jersey cream from Molly's milk made the pies "the best I ever ate," according to Walt, who not only milked Molly but also whipped the cream to its stiffness.

"Stay off the ice!" Judith Sampson called out to Mell and Paul as they raced outside to play after dinner.

Hannah watched the children leave, and she was peeved that Mell had gone out without helping to clean up after dinner. Hannah said nothing, though, and she pitched in to help while Walt went to the barn to feed the calves and Papa and Sam swapped hunting stories in the living room.

After some moments, Hannah peered out the

kitchen door to check on the children. What she saw terrified her.

"MAMA!" Hannah screamed. Not taking time for more words, she shot through the door and raced for the waterfront.

Mama was in the supply room, and Judith was in the bathroom.

Little Paul was on the ice at the end of the dock. He seemed to be enjoying himself, running and sliding.

"Paul, you'll break through the ice an' drown!" screamed big sister Mell. "Get off the ice right now!"

"Ain't gonna!" Paul flapped his chubby hands with his thumbs in his ears while he sticking his tongue out at Mell.

Mell swore.

Paul returned the profanity.

If she can only keep his attention a few minutes longer, raced through Hannah's harried brain. Hannah ran to where Papa's boats were overturned beside the dock and fished a skein of light nylon rope from underneath one of them. She made a loop in the rope as she ran out on the dock. She tossed the loop, and it dropped neatly over little Paul on the first try.

Hannah's eyes bulged in horror. Before Hannah could draw the loose rope tight and haul Paul off the ice, Paul had slipped the rope off his small shoulders, then had raced down the ice out of reach.

By this time, Sam was at the waterfront. He ran straight for his son, breaking the thin ice with his heavy boots. Sam was nearly there, struggling through water up to his armpits, when the cracks spread to Paul, who splashed headfirst into the icy lake within reach of his father.

Sam waded to shore, holding his son, kicking and screaming but unhurt.

"He broke the ice and made me fall in," Paul accused, pointing an angry finger at Sam. "He tried to drown me!"

But Judith had reached the porch before Sam got to Paul, and she had seen it all. "You're not going to lay it on your old man this time," she snapped. Grabbing his arm, she dragged Paul, still yelling, into the kitchen to towel him dry in front of Mama's wood-burning range. Sam went upstairs to change into clothes borrowed from Papa.

Angry and embarrassed at little Paul's outrageous conduct, Judith took her children and hurried for the old Sampson place as soon as Paul was dry.

Sam was badly shaken. He had saved his son's life. But Paul had only accused his father of trying to drown him.

"That woman disagrees with every attempt I make to straighten them kids out," Sam told Papa. "She's tryin' to turn 'em against me, seems like."

"Sounds like she took your side this time," Papa said.

Hannah, washing dishes, stopped to listen. She very much wanted to know why some families seem to get along so well while others were flying apart.

"For once," Sam agreed, "she saw what happened."

"Are you home most of the time?" Papa inquired.

"I don't guess my family saw me much until we moved to this island," Sam admitted. "There ain't no taverns on Beaver Island," he chuckled wryly.

"Then the kids may see you as a stranger. It may take seeing you at home every evening for a while to get used to you. Meanwhile, you need to work on your relationship with Judith."

"And I suppose I need to go to church," Sam said glumly. "Kids'r goin'. Judith's started goin' lately, too. I think it's done her good. She don't get mad so much. She ain't swore at me or the kids sence she got religion in Sunday school—that was two weeks ago."

"Well, there won't any of us get to church until this lake freezes solid enough to hold a snowmobile—that's a couple of weeks yet," Papa mused. "What you really need—what I expect Judith found in Sunday school—is a relationship with the One who created families. Jesus Christ died, shedding his blood, to pay for all the angry words, all the hard feelings, all the old grudges you and Judith and your kids are struggling with."

"It's that simple, is it? Just pray and ask Jesus to be my Savior?" said Sam, who had heard the gospel story before.

"Hey, you've heard!" Papa responded. "Now you need to believe. Ask Jesus to be Lord of your life and lift your burden. He'll give you a love for your family that you never imagined possible."

"And a 'peace and joy nothing can destroy.' I heard that song on the radio once. Harry, I want that peace," Sam declared at last.

Chapter Twenty

It Followed Her
To School One Day

Cheer for our team,
"Steamboaters" the name;
'Thout Hunter the houn' dog
We'd not be the same.

Hunter's our mascot,
This you must know;
He cheers us on when
He barks just so:
"WOOF, WOOF, WOOF!"

Laketon Christian Academy's six cheer-leaders yelled their heads off to the tune of the "Notre Dame Fight Song." "The Mascot Cheer," they called this new chorus, and Hunter was mascot—a very special hound dog indeed!

Hannah had received a very welcome letter right after Thanksgiving from her two friends in St. Louis, Mr. Parrish and Mr. Duke, who had salvaged the engine from the real steamboat, the *President*

Lincoln, which she and Walt had found at the bottom of Moosehead Lake. The letter said the men would donate the old Hardin Company warehouse to Laketon Community Church as a gym for Laketon Christian Academy. Since the *President Lincoln* had burned on the ice, the men had no more use for the warehouse. A good hardwood floor and bleachers, they said, would make it into a gym for the school's ball games.

"That's marvelous, darling," Mama exclaimed when she saw the letter. Papa showed the letter to their pastor, and within weeks the warehouse was being remodeled as a basketball gym.

"Easy, girl," murmured Hannah one evening, as Molly stepped around nervously during milking. Walt had finished feeding the calves and he was dribbling and doing layups on the barn's high-ceilinged floor in front of the tie-up where Molly was penned. The bouncing basketball made the cow nervous, though Hannah couldn't yell at Walt to stop, because that would frighten Molly even more.

"I'll speak to him." It was Papa, who had just stepped into the barn. He disappeared through the door to the barn floor, and the bouncing and dribbling stopped at once. Hannah could hear them talking in low tones as she finished milking.

"Where's Papa?" Mama wondered half an hour later. Though he walked with crutches, Papa kept busy at tasks where he could sit and use his tools. "He promised to look at the switch on my vacuum cleaner this evening," she fussed.

"Playing basketball with Walt, I guess," said Hannah. She had heard the bouncing begin again as she left the barn.

"But he'll hurt his leg!"

"Not likely." It was Walt coming into the lodge as Papa hobbled behind. "Papa's pretty good at foul shots from halfway across the barn, even on crutches," Walt laughed. "He didn't try to run, though. And guess what?" Walt sounded extremely pleased, Hannah thought.

"What?" Hannah and Mama asked in unison.

"Papa says I can join the academy's basketball team!" Walt was clearly elated.

"But you have no way to get there," protested Mama.

"I've got my truck. It'll go on the ice. Season ends about the time the lake thaws."

"But that takes gas." Mama knew well enough that Walt had spent most of his resources that fall on truck parts.

"I told Walt we'd buy the gas, so long's he's willing also to drive Hannah to the mainland whenever she needs to go to school for extra help," Papa put in.

Mama did not answer, but Hannah could tell by her knit brow that she was thinking, Gasoline costs money. Papa had had to let Sam Sampson keep the money paid by the hunters for guided trips, though Papa and Mama's small hotel business had done quite well entertaining hunting parties that fall.

"The Lord's been good to us," Papa continued. "It's only right that we let our kids expand their horizons once in a while." He carefully balanced his weight on one crutch so he could hug Mama.

"You're right," agreed Mama, smiling broadly. "And unless I'm tied down with guests, I'll be at the games yelling my head off for Walt!"

"Papa, it's too bad you've got a broken leg," Hannah sympathized, when she heard that several men from the church were laying a nice new maple floor to make the old warehouse into a gym. "It's our slack season here. You won't have much work to do until we get more tourists in the spring. You could help out."

"Come with me," Papa said, grinning.

Hannah followed him to his workshop. Here Papa showed her a low seat made of leather over a wooden frame. It had big casters, like a heavy footstool.

"I can sit on this and scoot around and nail floor boards down as fast as the fellows with two good legs," Papa chuckled.

After Papa had been driving to Laketon on the snowmobile to work on the gym floor for several days, Hannah and Walt took him to Laketon in Walt's truck. Walt, a freshman, was now on Laketon Christian Academy's basketball team. Hannah had gotten into some algebra problems that Mama couldn't help her with that week, so she had to get help from a teacher.

Walt and Hannah walked to the gym after school to see whether Papa was ready to go home to Beaver Island. To their surprise, Papa was one of *three* men scooting around on near-identical rolling seats as they nailed the floor down.

"Harry's Hurrier," the men called the device Papa had invented. "This floor is going down in record time," said the crew leader, a retired carpenter.

"That Caylin Coulson is really smitten with our Walt, I think," Papa said one January evening. Walt was in the barn taking his turn milking Molly, and

Hannah was in the kitchen paring northern spy apples for a pie. Mama had taken the dining room curtains down to launder that day, and Hannah noticed that the dining room with bare walls now carried her parents' voices from the living room like an echo chamber.

"You're probably right," agreed Mama, who had noticed that Walt and Caylin spent a lot of time together at church and Sunday school. "He left a letter on his chest of drawers. It smells of perfume, and the writing is in a *very* feminine hand."

"You didn't read it, I hope!" Having a son with a girlfriend was something new for Papa. But his own experience had taught him that personal letters are not to be nosed into, even when written to one's own son or daughter.

"I didn't even peek—I wouldn't think of it, Harry. But I shall suggest to Walt that he not put such temptations in my way again."

Deciding she'd probably heard too much, Hannah closed the kitchen door. Her parents' conversation about Walt was none of her business, she knew.

❋ ❋ ❋ ❋ ❋ ❋ ❋

"You stay here, boy," Hannah said as she hitched Hunter to Aunt Theresa's back porch one morning in January. "Auntie will let you in after a while."

Hannah was going to school twice a week now. On occasions when her schooldays were not the same as Walt's basketball practice, she spent the night with the Boudreaus and took Hunter along.

One day after lunch, Hannah's teacher, Mr. Robinson, had asked Jack, one of the students to empty the wastebasket. As Jack opened the door to the furnace room, a dog, which had evidently got in through an outside door left ajar by the custodian, shot out, knocking Jack off his feet. Hunter was at Hannah's desk before Jack could collect the contents of the wastebasket.

"Down, Hunter," Hannah whispered. Mr. Robinson was writing on the board and hadn't seen the hound come in.

Hunter lay on the floor in perfect obedience, but the seventh- and eighth-grade students began to snicker and make remarks.

"It seems that Hannah's little lamb is more obedient than some of our human class members," observed Mr. Robinson, who had now spotted Hunter.

Several girls stifled giggles.

"What shall I do with him, Mr. Robinson?" Hannah asked.

"It would take nearly until dismissal time for you to return him to your aunt's home at the waterfront," Mr. Robinson mused.

"Just put him outdoors," said Peter Monson, who didn't like dogs.

"He'd only whine and scratch until we had to let him back in," said Jennifer Earland, who loved dogs. "Besides, I think Hunter's cute."

"The class will return to order," Mr. Robinson admonished. "Hunter may remain if he's quiet," he added, to Hannah's astonishment.

※　※　※　※　※　※　※

On evenings when Laketon played home games, Hannah was usually there with Hunter. But a basketball court is quite a different place than a quiet classroom. When the cheering started, Hunter wanted to bark. Hannah found it quite a chore to keep her dog's snout clamped shut. During intermissions though, when the cheerleaders were shouting, nobody seemed to mind if Hunter barked, so long as he didn't cheer for the other side. Soon, the cheerleaders decided to make Hannah's hound their mascot.

"Look at what I found at ze Pet Centre in Skowhegan today, Hannah," Uncle Joe said a few days after a game in which Hunter had nearly gotten Hannah in trouble by barking at the wrong time. He pulled a plastic dog muzzle out of a package. The muzzle had a small box hanging from it.

"What is it?" It *did* look like an unusual muzzle. But why would Uncle Joe buy such a contraption for Hunter? Hannah was puzzled.

"This goes with it." Uncle Joe held up a device resembling a TV remote control, only smaller. "Let's try it out."

"Okay," Hannah shrugged. She trusted her uncle, and she knew he wouldn't hurt Hunter.

Uncle Joe strapped the muzzle onto Hunter and popped a nine-volt battery into the attached box, which tied easily in place with velcro straps. Then he put batteries into the special remote control.

"Now get a piece of cheese out of ze refrigerator. Tease him with it and make him bark," said Uncle Joe.

Hannah soon had Hunter barking and jumping about. Suddenly he stopped, mid-bark. Hunter shook his head in frustration. Hannah turned to Uncle Joe, who grinned at her.

"She is magic, *non?*" Uncle Joe pushed a button on the remote control, pointing it at Hunter.

Hunter started to bark again.

Uncle Joe pushed the button again.

Hunter stopped at once.

"How does it work, Uncle Joe?" Hannah cried.

"Ze box under his chin gives him a mild electric shock whenever he tries to bark," said Uncle Joe.

"And the remote control in your hand turns it on and off, like a TV set!" Hannah finished Uncle Joe's thought. "But isn't that kinda mean?"

"Not unless you pester the poor dumb beast and make him bark just to tease him," said Aunt Theresa. "Dogs *need* to learn manners."

"That's true," said Hannah, remembering the many times she'd had to get up at night to hush Hunter to keep him from disturbing Mama and Papa's guests.

Hunter the mascot quickly became a favorite at the basketball games. He wore a sweater of blue and gold, Laketon Christian Academy's school colors, which Hannah knit for him. At halftime, he was a sensation, barking with the cheers, clamping his mouth shut with a flash of Hannah's remote control. Hunter was soon known as the "electric dog."

❋ ❋ ❋ ❋ ❋ ❋ ❋

"She's *cute*." Hannah had heard the voice of that particular eighth-grade boy before. She was sitting with the cheerleaders at the ball game that evening, since she was needed to control Hunter.

None of the cheerleaders would look at the guy, Hannah told herself. They're all ninth graders or older.

"Aw, you say that about every new girl," another male voice said.

"I like her hair," said the first one.

Won't this guy ever quit? Hannah wondered. She shot a glance at Caylin, who was sitting next to her. Her hair was the most perfect Hannah had ever seen. The guys were talking about Caylin, Hannah was sure.

But Caylin's full attention was on the game. She hadn't heard the remarks behind her.

Hair. Hannah remembered her own long, strawberry blonde French braid, and she pulled it over her shoulder to retie the ribbon made of blue and gold yarn left over from Hunter's knit sweater.

"I'm going to ask her out," said the voice that had been describing a certain girl as "cute." "Since she's not a cheerleader, she won't be going to their party after the game."

Hannah knew that Walt had been invited. It was at Caylin Coulson's house, and the whole team would be there.

"She *may* go, y'know, man," said the other voice. "She's in charge of the team's mascot."

Hannah's ears burned. Collaring Hunter, Hannah got up to leave.

"Where y' goin'?" Caylin grabbed Hannah's sleeve. "There's a party at my house after, and you're invited."

※ ※ ※ ※ ※ ※ ※

"Mama, please come to my room," Hannah called softly at her parents' door. It was nearly midnight when Hannah and Walt returned to Beaver Lodge, driving across the frozen lake in Walt's truck two hours after their parents had gone home on the snowmobile.

Mama had not been asleep, and she quickly slipped into the bedroom with Hannah, who had changed into her pajamas before calling Mama.

"Mama, I want you to tuck me in and kiss me goodnight," Hannah murmured, crawling into bed.

Mama did so, then sat on Hannah's bed. "What's the matter, darling?" It had been many years since Hannah had asked to be tucked into bed.

"Mama, what does it mean when a guy is hitting on a girl?"

"Do you have any bruises?" Mama laughed.

"I don't mean *that* kind of hitting on—you know!"

"Yes, Hannah honey, I know." Mama smoothed Hannah's hair back. "I suppose it can mean as many different things as there are boys," said Mama. "Sometimes the girl just has to wait and see. Mostly, though, it means he likes you."

"What if the girl doesn't like the guy?"

"And what if the girl doesn't have anything against the guy? Maybe the girl just doesn't want guys to like her, period?" Mama asked a couple of questions of her own.

Hannah turned to peek at Mama out of the corner of her eye. "I s'pose you're right, Mama." Hannah sighed, thinking. "I guess I'll never understand myself," she said at last. "Monique and Millicent like boys—too much, I'm afraid. Caylin likes Walt, and I think that's sweet. But why did I get embarrassed when a guy said...said I was cute?"

"Because," Mama said plainly, "one part of you *wants* guys to think you're pretty. Another part of you is fearful of being liked by guys, because this means you're growing up. It's normal for a girl your age to be nervous around guys, I think."

"Maybe it's kinda like a baby's head," Hannah said, chuckling.

"How's that?" Mama was puzzled.

"When a baby is first born, its skull is in several parts. As the baby grows, its skull grows together. Maybe my mind is in two parts, and it just needs time to grow together. Then I'll understand these things."

"You're very perceptive. Just be sure your head grows as fast as your heart." Mama kissed Hannah again. "There is another ritual that we never missed at bedtime when you were small."

"I know, Mama." Hannah rolled over to face Mama and took her hand. "My turn to pray," she chirped. "Dear Jesus," Hannah prayed, "You know that I don't understand how I feel about guys. Please walk by my side and help me make the right choices. For Your name's sake. Amen."